V

OMICRON

Lincolnshire
COUNTY COUNCIL

discover libraries

This book should be returned on or before the due date.

NCI

11|15.

To renew or order library books please telephone 01522 782010
or visit https://lincolnshire.spydus.co.uk
You will require a Personal Identification Number.
Ask any member of staff for this.

The above does not apply to R

D1349908

05069860

VETTORI'S
DAMSEL
IN DISTRESS

VETTORI'S DAMSEL IN DISTRESS

BY

LIZ FIELDING

First published in Great Britain 2015
by Mills & Boon, an imprint of Harlequin (UK) Limited,
Large Print edition 2015
Eton House, 18-24 Paradise Road,
Richmond, Surrey, TW9 1SR

© 2015 Liz Fielding

ISBN: 978-0-263-25702-1

Printed and bound in Great Britain
by CPI Antony Rowe, Chippenham, Wiltshire

This book is dedicated to the authors
I hang out with online. They are the best
support group in the world—always up
for a brainstorming session when the plot
wobbles, ready to celebrate the good stuff
and reach out through cyberspace with
comfort when fate lobs lemons.

They know who they are.

CHAPTER ONE

'Life is like ice cream on a hot day. Enjoy it before it melts.'

—from *Rosie's Little Book of Ice Cream*

IT WAS LATE and throwing down a sleety rain when Geli emerged from the Metro at Porta Garibaldi into the Milan night. Her plan had been to take a taxi for the last short leg of her journey but it was par for the course, on a day when everything had conspired to keep her from her destination, that there wasn't one in sight.

Terrific.

The weather had been mild with a promise of spring in the air when she'd left Longbourne and, optimistically, she'd assumed Italy would be warmer; something to do with all those sun-soaked travel programmes on the television, no doubt. If she'd had the sense to check the local weather she'd have been wearing thermals instead of lace beneath her dress, leggings over her ultra-sheer black tights and a lot more than a lace choker around her neck.

Not the most practical outfit for travelling but she was going to Milan, style capital of Europe, where the inhabitants didn't wear joggers unless they were jogging and policewomen wore high heels.

In her determination to make a fashionable impression she had overlooked the fact that Milan was in the north of Italy. Where there were mountains. And, apparently, sleet.

Okaaay...

According to the details she'd downloaded from the Internet, her apartment was no more than a ten-minute stroll from the Metro. She could handle a bit of sleet. In style.

She checked her map and, having orientated herself, she pulled the wide hood of her coat over ears that were beginning to tingle, shouldered her roomy leather tote and, hauling her suitcase behind her, set off.

New country, new start, new life.

Unlike her sisters, who were married, raising families and, with their rapidly expanding ice cream events business, had life all sewn up and sorted, she was throwing herself into the dark—literally.

With little more than an Italian phrasebook and a head full of ideas, she was setting out to grab every experience that life offered her. If, as she crossed the railway bridge into the unknown, the thrill of nervous excitement that shot through her was edged with a ripple of apprehension, a shiver of fear—well, that was perfectly natural. She was the baby of the family.

She might be the one with the weird clothes, the 'attitude', but they knew it was all front; that this was her first time out in the world. Okay, she'd been to Italy before, but that was on a student study trip and she'd been with a group of people she knew. This time she was on her own, without the family safety net of loving hands reaching out to steady her if she stumbled. To catch her if she fell. Testing herself…

'*Scusi!*'

'Sorry…um…*scusi*…' She steered her case to one side to let someone in a hurry pass her and then, as she looked up, she saw the colourful street art gleaming under the street lights—bright tropical scenes that lit up dull concrete—and caught her breath.

Despite the icy stuff stinging her face, excitement won out as she remembered why she had chosen Italy, Milan... Isola.

The minute she'd opened a magazine, seen the photographs, read about this enclave of artists, musicians, designers all doing their own thing, she'd been hooked. This was a place where she could spread her wings, explore her love of fashion, seek new ways of making art and maybe, just maybe fall in love. Nothing serious, not for keeps, but for fun.

Twenty minutes later, her face stiff with cold, the freezing stuff finding its way into a hood designed more for glamour than protection, and totally lost, the bounce had left her step.

She could almost see her oldest sister, Elle, shaking her head and saying, *You're so impatient, Geli! Why didn't you wait for a taxi?*

Because it was an *adventure*! And the directions had been simple enough. She'd counted the turnings, checked the name of the street, turned right and her apartment should be there, right in front of her, on the corner.

Except it wasn't.

Instead of the pink-painted five-storey house on the corner of a street of equally pretty houses that overlooked the twice-weekly market, she was faced with eight-feet-high wooden barriers surrounding a construction site.

No need to panic. Obviously she'd missed a turning. There had been a couple of narrow openings—more alleys than streets—that she'd thought were too small to be the turnings on her map. Obviously she was wrong.

She backtracked, recounted and headed down one just about wide enough to take a Fiat 500. It ended in a tiny courtyard piled up with crates and lit by a dim lamp over what looked like the back entrance to a shop. In the dark something moved, a box fell, and she beat a hasty retreat.

The few people about had their heads down and her, *'Scusi...'* was blown away on wind that was driving the sleet, thicker now, into her face.

It was time to take another look at the map.

Ducking into the shelter of the doorway of a shuttered shop, she searched her tote for the powerful mini torch given to her by her explorer brother-in-law as a parting gift.

She'd reminded him that she was going to one of the world's great cities rather than venturing into the jungle. His response was that in his experience there was little difference and as something wet and hairy brushed against her leg she let out a nervous shriek.

Make that one for the explorer.

A plaintive mew reassured her and the bright beam of her torch picked out a tiny kitten, wet fur sticking to its skin, cowering in the doorway.

'Hey, sweetie,' she said softly, reaching out to it, but it backed away nervously. She knew how it felt. 'You're much too little to be out by yourself on a night like this.'

The poor creature, wetter and certainly colder than she was, mewed pitifully in agreement. She'd bought a cheese sandwich on the plane but had been too churned up with nerves and excitement to eat it and she opened it up, broke a piece off and offered it to the kitten. Hunger beat fear and it snatched the food from her fingers, desperately licking at the butter.

Geli broke off another piece and then turned her attention to the simple street map. Clearly she'd taken a wrong turn and wandered into the commercial district, now closed for the night, but for the life of her couldn't see where she'd gone wrong.

Phoning Signora Franco, her landlady, was not an option. The *signora*'s English was about on a par with her own Italian—enthusiastic, but short on delivery. What she needed was one of Isola's famous cafés or bars, somewhere warm and dry with people who would know the area and, bracing herself to face to what was now whiter, more solid than mere sleet, she peered along the street.

Behind her, the kitten mewed and she sighed. There were a few lights on in upper floors but down here everything was shut up. The tiny creature was on its own and was too small to survive the night without shelter. The location might be new, but some things never changed.

Inevitably, having begged for help, the kitten panicked when she bent and scooped it up but she eased it into one of the concealed seam pockets hidden amongst the full layers of her coat.

She'd come back tomorrow and see if she could find someone who'd take responsibility for it but right now it was time to put her Italian to the test. She'd memorised the question and could rattle off *'Dov'è* Via Pepone?' without a second thought. Understanding the answers might be more of a problem.

She stuffed her torch, along with the useless map, in her bag and began to retrace her steps back to the road from the station, this time carrying straight on instead of turning off.

In the photographs she'd seen it had been summer; there were open-air jazz concerts, the communal garden and collective 'bring a dish' lunches where every Tuesday the local people gathered to share food and reinforce the community ties. People sitting outside trendy cafés. Perfect.

This was the wrong time of day, the wrong time of year. Even the famous Milan 'promenade' was on hold but, encouraged by a sudden snatch of music—as if someone had opened a door very briefly—she hurried to the corner and there, on the far side of a piazza, lights shone through a steamy window.

It was Café Rosa, famous for jazz, cocktails and being a hangout of local artists who used the walls as a gallery. More relieved than she cared to admit, she slithered across the cobbles and pushed open the door.

She was immediately swathed in warmth, the rich scent of luscious food and cool music from a combo on a tiny stage in the corner mingling with bursts of steam from the expresso machine. Tables of all shapes and sizes were filled with people eating, drinking, gossiping, and a tall dark-haired man was leaning against the counter talking to the barista.

If the scene had been posed by the Italian Tourist Board it couldn't have been more perfect and, despite the cold, she felt a happy little rush of anticipation.

A few people had turned when the door opened and the chatter died away until the only sound was the low thrum of a double bass.

The man standing at the bar, curious about what had caught everyone's attention, half turned and anticipation whooshed off the scale in an atavistic charge of raw desire; instant, bone-deep need for a man before you heard his voice, felt his touch, knew his name.

For a moment, while she remembered how to breathe, it felt as if someone had pressed the pause button on the scene, freezing the moment in soft focus. Muted colours reflected in polished steel, lights shimmering off the bottles and glasses behind the bar, her face reflected, ghost-like, behind the advertisement on a mirror. And Mr Italy with his kiss-me mouth and come-to-bed eyes.

Forget the thick dark hair and cheekbones sharp

enough to write their own modelling contract, it was those chocolate-dark eyes that held her transfixed. If they had been looking out of a tourist poster there would be a stampede to book holidays in Italy.

He straightened, drawing attention to the way his hair curled onto his neck, a pair of scandalously broad shoulders, strong wrists emerging from folded-back cuffs.

'*Signora...*' he murmured as he moved back a little to make room for her at the counter and, oh, joy, his voice matched the face, the body.

She might have passed out for lack of oxygen at that moment but a tall, athletic-looking blonde placed a tiny cup of espresso in front of him before—apparently unaware that she was serving a god—turning to her.

'*Sta nevicando? E brutto tempo.*'

What?

Oh...

Flustered at being confronted with phrases that hadn't featured so far on the Italian course she'd downloaded onto her iPod, she took the safe option and, having sucked in a snowflake that was clinging to her lip, she lowered her hood. The chatter gradually resumed and, finally getting a *move it* message through to her legs, she parked her suitcase and crossed to the bar.

 'Cosa prendi, signora?'

Oh, whew, something she understood. 'Um... *Vorrai un espresso...s'il vous plait...'* Her answer emerged in a mangled mixture of English, Italian and French. 'No...I mean...' *Oh, heck.*

The blonde grinned. 'Don't worry. I got the gist,' she replied, her English spiced with an Australian accent.

'Oh, thank goodness you're English. No! Sorry, Australian—' Achingly conscious of the man leaning against the counter, an impressive thigh stretching the cloth of his jeans just inches from her hip, she attempted to recover the cool, sophisticated woman of the world image with which she'd intended to storm Milan. 'Shall I go out, walk around the block and try that again?'

The woman grinned. 'Stay right where you are. I'll get that espresso. You've just arrived in Isola?' she asked as she measured the coffee.

'In Isola, in Milan, in Italy. I've been working on my Italian—I picked some up when I spent a month in Tuscany as a student—but I learned French at school and it seems to be my brain's foreign language default setting when I panic.'

Her brain was too busy drooling over Mr Italy to give a toot.

'Give it a week,' the woman said. 'Can I get you anything else?'

'A side order of directions?' she asked hopefully, doing her best to ignore the fact that it wasn't just her brain; her entire body was responding on a visceral level to the overdose of pheromones wafting in her direction. It was like being bombarded by butterflies. Naked…

She was doing her level best not to stare at him.

Was he looking at her?

'You are lost, *signora*?' he asked.

In Italian, his voice was just about the sexiest thing she'd ever heard, but his perfect, lusciously accented English sent a shiver rippling down her spine that had nothing to do with the snow dripping from her hair. That was trickling between her breasts and turning to steam.

She took a breath and, doing her best to remember why she was there, said, 'Not lost exactly…' Retrieving the apartment details from her tote, she placed it, map side up, on the counter and turned to him, intending to explain what had happened. He was definitely looking and, confronted with those eyes, the questioning kink of his brow, language of any description deserted her.

'No?' he prompted.

Clearly he was used to women losing the power of speech in his presence. From the relaxed way he was leaning against the bar, to eyes that, with one look made her feel as if he owned her, everything about him screamed danger.

First day in Isola and she could imagine having a lot of fun with Mr Italy and, from the way he was looking at her, he was thinking much the same thing about her.

Was that how it had been for her mother that first time? One look from some brawny roustabout at the annual village fair and she'd been toast?

'I know exactly where I am, *signor*,' she said, looking into those lusciously dark eyes. To emphasise the point she eased off the fine leather glove that had done little to keep her hand warm and tapped the piazza with the tip of a crimson nail.

'No,' he repeated, and this time it wasn't a question as, never taking his eyes from hers, he wrapped long fingers around her hand and moved her finger two inches to the right. 'You are here.'

His hand was warm against her cold skin. On the surface everything was deceptively still but inside, like a volcano on the point of blowing, she was liquid heat.

She fought the urge to swallow. 'I am?'

She was used to people staring at her. From the age of nine she had been the focus of raised eyebrows and she'd revelled in it.

This man's look was different. It sizzled through her and, afraid that the puddle of snow melting at her feet was about to turn to steam, she turned to the map.

It didn't help. Not one bit. His hand was still covering hers, long ringless fingers darkly masculine against her own pale skin, and she found herself wondering how they would look against her breast. How they would feel…

Under the layers of black—coat, dress, the lace of her bra—her nipples hardened in response to her imagination, sending touch-me messages to all parts south and she bit on her lower lip to stop herself from whimpering.

Breathe, breathe…

She cleared the cobwebs from her throat and, hoping she sounded a lot more in control than she was, said, 'One piazza looks very much like another on a map. Unfortunately, neither of them is where I was going.'

'And yet here you are.'

And yet here she was, falling into eyes as dark as the espresso in his cup.

The café retreated. The bright labels on bottles behind the bar, the clatter of cutlery, the low thrum of a double bass became no more than a blur of colour, sound. All her senses were focused on the touch of his fingers curling about her hand, his molten eyes reflecting back her own image. For a moment nothing moved until, abruptly, he turned away and used the hand that had been covering hers to pick up his espresso and drain it in one swallow.

He'd looked away first and she waited for the rush of power that always gave her but it didn't come. For the first time in her life it didn't feel like a victory.

Toast...

'Where are you going, *signora*?' He carefully replaced the tiny cup on its saucer.

'Here...' She looked down but the ink had run, leaving a dirty splodge where the name of the street had been.

'Tell him the address and Dante will point you

in the right direction,' the barista said, putting an espresso in front of her. 'He knows every inch of Isola.'

'Dante?' Geli repeated. 'As in the *Inferno*?' No wonder he was so hot... Catching the barista's knowing grin, she quickly added, 'Or perhaps your mother is an admirer of the Pre-Raphaelites?'

'Are you visiting someone?' he asked, ignoring the question.

'No.' Mentally kicking herself for speaking before her brain was in gear—he must have heard that one a thousand times—she shook her head. 'I'm here to work. I've leased an apartment for a year. Geli Amery,' she added, offering him her hand without a thought for the consequences.

He wrapped his hand around hers and held it.

'Dante Vettori.' Rolled out in that sexy Italian accent, his name was a symphony of seduction. 'Your name is Jelly?' He lifted an eyebrow, but not like the disapproving old biddies in the village shop. Not at all. 'Like the wobbly stuff the British inflict on small children at birthday parties?'

Okay, so she'd probably asked for that with her

stupid *'Inferno'* remark, but he wasn't the only one to have heard it all before.

'Or add to peanut butter in a sandwich if you're American?' She lifted an eyebrow right back at him, which was asking for trouble but who knew if he'd ever lift his eyebrow at her like that again? This was definitely one of those 'live for the day' moments she had vowed to grab with both hands and she was going for it.

'é possíbile,' he said, the lines bracketing his mouth deepening into a smile. 'But I suspect not.'

He could call her what he liked as long as he kept smiling like that...

'You suspect right. Geli is short for Angelica—as in *angelica archangelica*, which I'm told is a very handsome plant.' And she smiled back. 'You may be more familiar with its crystallised stem. The British use it to decorate the cakes and trifles that they inflict on small children at birthday parties.'

His laugh was rich and warm, creating a fan of creases around his eyes, emphasising those amazing cheekbones, widening his mouth and drawing attention to a lower lip that she wanted to lick...

Make that burnt toast...

In an attempt to regain control of her vital organs, Geli picked up her espresso and downed it in a single swallow, Italian style. It was hotter than she expected, shocking her out of the lusty mist.

'I had intended to take a taxi—' Her vocal cords were still screaming from the hot coffee and the words came out as little more than a squeak. She cleared her throat and tried again. 'Unfortunately, there were none at the Porta Garibaldi and on the apartment details it said that Via Pepone was only a ten-minute walk.'

'Taxis are always in short supply when the weather's bad,' the barista said, as Dante, frowning now, turned the details over to look at the picture of the pretty pink house where she'd be living for the next year. 'Welcome to Isola, Geli. Lisa Vettori—I'm from the Australian branch of the family. Dante's my cousin and, although you wouldn't know it from the way he's lounging around on the wrong side of the counter, Café Rosa is his bar.'

'I pay you handsomely so that I can stay on this side of the bar,' he reminded her, without looking up.

'Make the most of it, mate. I have a fitting for a

bridesmaid dress in Melbourne on Tuesday. Unless you get your backside in gear and find a temp to take my place, come Sunday you'll be the one getting up close and personal with the Gaggia.' She took a swipe at the marble counter top with a cloth to remove an invisible mark. 'Have you got a job lined up, Geli?' she asked.

'A job?'

'You said you were here to work. Have you ever worked in a bar? Only there's a temporary—'

'If you've been travelling all day you must be hungry,' Dante said, cutting his cousin off in mid-sentence. 'We'll have the risotto, Lisa.' And, holding onto the details of her apartment and, more importantly, the map, he headed for a table for two that was tucked away in a quiet corner.

CHAPTER TWO

'There's nothing more cheering than a good friend when you're in trouble—except a good friend with ice cream.'

—from *Rosie's Little Book of Ice Cream*

TOO SURPRISED TO REACT, Geli didn't move. Okay, so there had been some fairly heavy-duty flirting going on, but that was a bit arrogant—

Dante pulled out a chair and waited for her to join him.

Make that quite a lot arrogant. Did he really think she would simply follow him?

'Angelica?'

No one used her full name, but he said it with a 'g' so soft that it felt like chocolate melting on her tongue and while her head was still saying, *Oh, please...*her body went to him as if he'd tugged a chain.

'Give me your coat,' he said, 'and I'll hang it up to dry.'

She swallowed.

It was late. She should be on her way but for that she needed directions, which was a good, practical reason to do as he said. Then again, nothing that had happened since she'd walked through the door of Café Rosa had been about the practicalities and, letting her tote slide from her shoulder onto the chair, she dropped her glove on the table and began to tug at its pair.

Warm now, the fine leather clung to her skin and as she removed her glove, one finger at a time, Geli discovered that there was more than one way of being in control.

A chain had two ends and now Dante was the one being hauled in as she slowly revealed her hand with each unintentionally provocative tug.

She dropped the glove beside its pair and everything—the heartbeat pounding in her ears, her breathing—slowed right down as, never taking her eyes off his, she lowered her hand and, one by one, began to slip the small jet buttons that nipped her coat into her waist.

There were a dozen of them and, taking her time, she started at the bottom. One, two, three… His gaze never wavered for a second until the bias cut swathes of velvet, cashmere and butter-soft suede—flaring out in layers that curved from just below her knees at the front to her heels at the back—fell open to reveal the black scoop-necked mini-dress that stopped four inches above her knees.

She waited a heartbeat and then turned and let the coat slip from her shoulders, leaving him to catch it.

An arch *got you* lift of an eyebrow as she thanked him should leave him in no doubt that the next move was up to him and she was more than ready for anything he had to offer, but as she glanced over her shoulder, fell into the velvet softness of his eyes, she forgot the plot.

He was so close. His breath was warm on her cheek, his mouth was inches away and her eyebrow stayed put as she imagined closing the gap and taking his delicious lower lip between hers.

Make that burned to a crisp toast. Toast about to burst into flames…

She blinked as a clatter of cutlery shattered the moment and Dante looked down at her coat as if wondering where it had come from.

'I'll hang this by the heater to dry,' he said.

'Are you mad?' Lisa, the table swiftly laid, took it from him. 'You don't hang something like this over a radiator as if it's any old chain store rain-coat. This kind of quality costs a fortune and it needs tender loving care.' She checked the label. 'Dark Angel.' She looked up. 'Angel?' she repeated and then, with a look of open admiration, 'Is that you, Geli?'

'What? Oh, yes,' she said, grateful for the distraction. Falling into bed for fun with a man was one thing. Falling into anything else was definitely off the agenda... 'Dark Angel is my label.'

'You're a fashion designer?'

'Not exactly. I make one-off pieces. I studied art but I've been making clothes all my life and somehow I've ended up combining the two.'

'Clothes as art?' She grinned. 'I like it.'

'Let's hope you're not the only one.'

'Not a chance. This is absolutely lush. Did you make the choker, too?' she asked. 'Or is that an original?'

'If only...' Geli touched the ornate Victorian-style lace and jet band at her throat. 'It's recycled from stuff in my odds and ends box. I cut my dress from something I found on the "worn once" rack at the church jumble sale and—' if she kept talking she wouldn't grab Dante Vettori

'—my coat was made from stuff I've collected over the years.'

'Well…wow. You are so going to fit in here. Upcycling is really big in Isola.'

'It's one of the reasons I'm here. I want to work with people who are doing the same kind of thing.'

'And I suggested you might want a job behind the bar.' She rolled her eyes. 'If you've got something you want to exhibit I'm sure Dan will find space for it.' She glanced at him, but he offered no encouragement. 'Right, well, I'll go and find a hanger for this,' she said, holding the coat up so that it didn't touch the floor. She'd only gone a couple of steps when she stopped. 'Geli, there's something moving… Omigod!' She screamed and, forgetting all about its lushness, dropped the coat and leapt back. 'It's a rat!'

The musicians stopped playing mid-note. The patrons of the café, who had resumed chatting, laughing, eating, turned as one.

Then the kitten, confused, frightened, bolted across the floor and pandemonium broke out as men leapt to their feet and women leapt on chairs.

'It's all right!' Geli yelled as she dived under a table to grab the kitten before some heavy-footed male stamped on the poor creature. Terrified, it scratched and sank its little needle teeth deep into the soft pad of her thumb before she emerged with it grasped in her hand. 'It's a kitten!' Then, in desperation when that didn't have any effect, *'Uno kitty!'*

She held it up so that everyone could see. It had dried a little in the shelter of her pocket but it was a scrawny grey scrap, not much bigger than her hand. No one looked convinced and, when a woman let loose a nervous scream, Dante hooked his arm around her waist and swept her and the kitten through the café to a door that led to the rear.

As it swung shut behind him the sudden silence was brutal.

'Uno kitty?' Dante demanded, looming over her. Much too close.

'I don't know the Italian for kitten,' she said, shaken by the speed at which events had overtaken her.

'It's *gattino*, but Lisa is right, that wretched creature looks more like a drowned rat.'

And the one word you didn't want to hear if you were in the catering business was *rat*.

'I'm sorry but I found it shivering in a doorway.

It was soaking wet. Freezing. I couldn't leave it there.'

'Maybe not—' he didn't look convinced '—but rats, cats, it's all the same to the health police.'

'I understand. My sisters are in the catering business.' And in similar circumstances they would have killed her. 'I only stopped to ask for directions. I didn't mean to stay for more than a minute or two.'

Epic distraction…

She was about to repeat her apology when the door opened behind them. Dante dropped his arm from her waist as Lisa appeared with her coat and bag over one arm and trailing her suitcase, leaving a cold space.

'Have you calmed them down?' he asked.

'Nothing like free drinks all round to lighten the mood. Bruno is dealing with it.'

Geli groaned. 'It's my fault. I'll pay for them.'

'No…' Lisa and Dante spoke as one then Lisa added, 'The first rule of catering is that if you see a rat, you don't scream. The second is that you don't shout, *It's a rat*… Unfortunately, when I felt something move and that something was grey and furry I totally— Omigod, Geli, you're bleeding!'

Geli glanced at the trickle of blood running down her palm. 'It's nothing. The poor thing panicked.'

'A poor thing that's been who knows where,' Lisa replied, 'eating who knows what filth. Come on, we'll go upstairs and I'll clean it up for you.'

'It's okay, honestly,' Geli protested, now seriously embarrassed. 'It's late and Signora Franco, the woman who owns the apartment I've rented, will be waiting for me with the key. I would have called her to let her know my plane had been delayed but her English is even worse than my Italian.'

Geli glanced at her watch. She'd promised to let her sisters know when she was safely in her apartment and it was well past ten o'clock. She'd warned them that her plane had been delayed but if she didn't text them soon they'd be imagining all sorts.

'There's no need to worry about Signora Franco,' Dante said.

'Oh, but—'

'Via Pepone has been demolished to make way for an office block,' he said, his expression grim. 'I hoped to break it to you rather more gently, but I'm afraid the apartment you have rented no longer exists.'

It took a moment for what Dante had said to sink in. There was no Via Pepone? No apartment? 'But I spoke to Signora Franco…'

'Find a box for Rattino, Lis, before he does any more damage.' Dante took her coat and bag from his cousin and ushered her towards the stairs.

Geli didn't move. This had to be a mistake. 'Maybe I have the name of the street wrong?' she said, trying not to think about how the directions on the map she'd been sent had taken her to a construction site. 'Maybe it's a typo—'

'Let's get your hand cleaned up. Are your tetanus shots up to date?' he asked.

'What? Oh, yes…' She stood her ground for another ten seconds but she couldn't go back into the restaurant with the kitten and if there was a problem with the apartment she had to know. And Lisa was right—the last thing she needed was an infected hand.

Concentrate on that. And repeating her apology wouldn't hurt.

'I really am sorry about the rat thing,' she said as she began to climb the stairs. 'The kitten really would have died if I'd left it out there.'

'So you picked it up and put it in the pocket of your beautiful coat?' He liked her coat… 'Do you do that often?'

'All the time,' she admitted. 'Coat pockets, bags, the basket of my bicycle. My sisters did their best to discourage me, but eventually they gave it up as a lost cause.'

'And are they always this ungrateful? Your little strays?' As they reached the landing he took her hand in his to check the damage and Geli forgot about the kitten, her apartment, pretty much everything as the warmth of his fingers seeped beneath her skin and into the bone.

When she didn't answer, he looked up and the temperature rose to the point where she was blushing to her toes.

Toast in flames. Smoke alarm hurting her eardrums…

'Frightened animals lash out,' she said quickly, waiting for him to open one of the doors, but he kept her hand in his and headed up a second flight of stairs.

There was only one door at the top. He let go of her hand, took a key from his pocket, unlocked it and pushed it open, standing back so that she could go ahead of him.

Geli wasn't sure what she'd expected; she hadn't actually been doing a lot of thinking since he'd turned and looked at her. Her brain had been working overtime dealing with the bombardment of her senses—new sights, new scents, a whole new level of physical response to a man.

Maybe a staff restroom…

Or maybe not.

There was a small entrance hall with hooks for coats, a rack for boots. Dante hung her coat beside a worn waxed jacket then opened an inner door to a distinctly masculine apartment.

There were tribal rugs from North Africa on the broad planks of a timber floor gleaming with the patina of age, splashes of brilliantly coloured modern art on the walls, shelves crammed with books. There was the warm glow and welcoming scent of logs burning in a wood stove and an enormous old leather sofa pulled up invitingly in front of it. The kind with big rounded arms—perfect for curling up against—and thick squashy cushions.

'You live here,' she said stupidly.

'Yes.' His face was expressionless as he tossed her bag onto the sofa. 'I'm told that it's very lower middle class to live over the shop but it suits me.'

'Well, that's just a load of tosh.'

'Tosh?' he repeated, as if he'd never heard the word before. Maybe he hadn't but it hardly needed explaining. It was all there in the sound.

'Total tosh. One day I'm going to live in a house exactly like this,' she said, turning around so that she could take in every detail. 'The top floor for me, workshops on the floor below me and a showroom on the ground floor—' she came to halt, facing him '—and my great-grandfather was the younger son of an earl.'

'An earl?'

Realising just how pompous that must have sounded, Geli said, 'Of course my grandmother defied her father and married beneath her, so we're not on His Lordship's Christmas card list, which may very well prove the point. Not that they're on ours,' she added.

'They disowned her?'

She shrugged. 'Apparently they had other, more obedient children.'

And that was more personal information than she'd shared with anyone, ever, but she didn't want him to think any of them gave a fig for their aristocratic relations. Even *in extremis* they'd never turned to them for help.

'The family, narrow-minded and full of secrets, is the source of all our discontents,' Dante replied, clearly quoting someone.

'Who said that?' she asked.

'I just did.'

'No, I meant…' She shook her head. He knew exactly what she meant. 'I have a great family.' For years it had just been the four of them. Her sisters, Elle and Sorrel, and their grandmother. They'd been solid. A tight-knit unit standing against the world. That had all changed the day a stranger had arrived on the doorstep with an ice cream van. Now her sisters were not only successful businesswomen, but married and producing babies as if they were going out of fashion, while Great-Uncle Basil—who'd sent the van— and Grandma were warming their old bones in the south of France.

'You are very fortunate.'

'Yes…' If you ignored the empty space left by her mother. By an unknown father. By the legions of aunts, uncles, cousins that she didn't know. Who didn't know her.

'The bathroom is through here,' Dante said, opening a door to an inner hall.

'*Il bagno…*' she said brightly, making an effort

to think in Italian as she followed him. Making an effort to think.

His *bagno* would, in estate agent speak, have been described as a 'roomy vintage-style' bathroom. In this case she was pretty certain the fittings—a stately roll-top bath with claw feet and gleaming brass taps, a loo with a high tank and a wide, deep washbasin—were the real deal.

'I'll shut the door so that you can put the kitten down,' he said, and the roominess shrank in direct proportion to the width of his shoulders as he shut the door. 'He can't escape.'

'I wouldn't bank on it,' she said as, carefully unhooking the creature's claws from the front of her dress, she set it down in the bath. 'And if it went under the *bagno*...' She left him to imagine what fun it would be trying to tempt him out.

Dante glanced down as the kitten, a tiny front paw resting against the steep side of the bath, protested at this indignity. 'Smart thinking.'

'When you've taken a room apart looking for a kitten that's managed to squeeze through a crack in the skirting board,' she told him, 'you learn to keep them confined.'

'You live an interesting life, Angelica Amery,' he said, watching as she attempted to slip the buttons at her wrist without getting blood on her dress.

'Isn't that a curse in China?' she asked.

'I believe that would be "May you live in interesting times",' he said, 'but you'll forgive me if I say that you don't dress like a woman in search of a quiet life.'

'Well, you know what they say,' she replied. 'Life is short. Eat ice cream every day.'

A smile deepened the lines bracketing his mouth, fanned out from his eyes. 'What "they" would that be?'

'More of an "it", actually. It's Rosie, our vintage ice cream van. In her *Little Book of Ice Cream*.' He looked confused—who wouldn't? 'Of course she has a vested interest.'

'Right...'

'It's the sentiment that matters, Dante. You can substitute whatever lifts your spirits. Chocolate? Cherries?' No response. 'Cheese?' she offered, hoping to make him laugh. Or at least smile.

'Permesso?' He indicated her continuing struggle with shaky fingers and fiddly buttons.

Okay, it wasn't that funny and, giving up on the buttons, she surrendered her hand. *'Prego.'*

He carefully unfastened the loops holding the

cuff together, folded the sleeve back out of the way, then, taking hold of her wrist, he pumped a little liquid soap into her palm.

Her heart rate, which was already going well over the speed limit, accelerated and, on the point of telling him that she could handle it from here, she took her own advice. Okay, it wasn't ice cream or even chocolate, but how often was a seriously scrumptious man going to take her hand between his and—?

'*Coraggio*,' he murmured as his thumb brushed her palm and a tiny whimper escaped her lips.

'Mmm…'

He turned to look at her, the edge of his faintly stubbled jaw an enticing whisper away from her lips. 'Does that sting?'

'No…' She shook her head. 'That's not…stinging.'

She was feeling no pain as he gently massaged the soap between her fingers, around her thumb, wrist and into her palm. All sensation was centred much lower as he rinsed off the soap, pulled a thick white towel from a pile and carefully dried her hand.

'*Va bene?*' he asked.

'*Va bene,*' she repeated. Very, very *bene* indeed. He was so deliciously gentle. So very *thorough*.

'Hold on. This *will* sting,' he warned as he took a box of antiseptic wipes from the cupboard over the sink and opened a pouch.

'I'll try not to scream,' she said but, taking no chances—her knees were in a pitifully weak state—she did as she was told and, putting her other hand on his shoulder, hung on.

She'd feel such a fool if she collapsed at his feet. *Really.*

His shoulder felt wonderfully solid beneath the soft wool shirt. He was so close that she was breathing in the scent of coffee, warm male skin and, as his hair slid in a thick silky wedge over his forehead, she took a hit of the herby shampoo he used. It completely obliterated the sharp smell of antiseptic.

He opened a dressing and applied it carefully to the soft mound of flesh beneath her thumb.

'All done.'

'No…'

Dante looked up, a silent query buckling the space between his brows and her mouth dried. He'd been right about the need to hang on. The word had slipped through her lips while her brain was fully occupied in keeping her vertical.

'There's something else?' he asked.

'Yes... No...' She hadn't been criticising his first aid skills; she just hadn't wanted him to stop. 'It's nothing.'

'Tell me,' he pressed her, all concern.

What on earth could she say? The answer that instantly popped into her mind was totally outrageous but Dante was waiting and she managed a careless little shrug and waited for him to catch on.

Nothing...

For heaven's sake, everyone knew what you did when someone hurt themselves. Did she have to spell it out for him?

'Un bacio?' she prompted.

'A kiss?' he repeated, no doubt wondering if she had the least clue what she was saying.

'Sì...' It was in an Italian phrasebook that her middle sister, Sorrel, had bought her. Under 'People', sub-section 'Getting Intimate', which she'd found far more engrossing than the section on buying a train ticket.

Posso baciarti?—Can I kiss you?—was there, along with other such useful phrases as *Can I buy you a drink?*, *Let's go somewhere quieter* and *Stop bothering me!*

There hadn't been a phrase for kissing it better. Perhaps it was in the 'Health' section.

'This is considered beneficial?' Dante asked.

He was regarding her with such earnestness that Geli wished the floor would just open up and swallow her. Then the flicker of a muscle at the corner of his mouth betrayed him and she knew that Dante Vettori had been teasing her. That he'd known exactly what she meant. That it was going to be all right. Better than all right— the man wasn't just fabulous to look at; he had a sense of humour.

'Not just beneficial,' she assured him. 'It's absolutely essential.'

'Forgive me. I couldn't have been paying attention when this was covered in first aid,' he said, the muscle working overtime to contain the smile fighting to break out. 'You may have to show me.'

Show him? Excitement rippled through her at the thought. It was outrageous but a woman in search of an interesting life had to seize the day. Lick the ice cream—

Coraggio, Geli—

'It's very simple, Dante. You just put your lips together—'

'Like this?'

She caught her breath as he raised her hand and, never taking his eyes from hers, touched his lips to the soft mound of her palm, just below the dressing he'd applied with such care.

'Exactly like that,' she managed through a throat that felt as if it had been stuffed with silk chiffon. 'I'm not sure why it works—'

'I imagine it's to do with the application of heat,' he said, his voice as soft as the second warm kiss he breathed into her palm. Her knees turned to water and her hand slid from his shoulder to clutch a handful of shirt. Beneath it, she could feel the thud of his heartbeat—a slow, steady counterpoint to her own racing pulse. 'Is that hot enough?'

Was he still teasing? The threatened smile had never appeared but his mouth was closer. Much closer.

'The more heat,' she murmured, her words little more than a whisper, 'the more effective the cure.'

'How hot do you want it to be, Angelica?' His voice trickled over her skin like warm honey and his eyes were asking the question that had been there since he'd turned and looked at her. Since he'd put his hand on hers and moved it across the map.

His hand was at her back now, supporting her, his breath soft against her lips and her answer was to lift the hand he'd kissed, slide her fingers through his dark silky hair. This close, she could see that the velvet dark of his irises was shot through with tiny gold sparks, sparks that arced between them, igniting some primitive part of her brain.

'Hot,' she murmured. *'Molto, molto caldo...'* And she touched his luscious lower lip with her mouth, her tongue, sucking in the taste of rich dark coffee that lingered there. Maybe it was the caffeine—on her tongue on his—but, as she closed her eyes and he angled his mouth to deepen the kiss, cradled her head, she felt a zingy hyper-tingle of heat lick through her veins, seep into her skin, warming her, giving her life.

'Hello?' Lisa's voice filtered through the golden mist. 'Everything okay?' she called, just feet from the bathroom door and, from the urgency with which she said it, Geli suspected that it wasn't the first time she'd asked.

Geli opened her eyes as Dante raised his head, took a step back, steadying her as a cold space opened up between them where before there had been closeness, heat.

'Don't open the door or the kitten will escape,' he warned sharply.

'Right… I just meant to tell you that there are antiseptic wipes in the cabinet.'

'I found them.' His hand slid from her shoulder and he reached for the door handle. 'We're all done.'

Noooo… But he'd already opened the door and stepped through it, closing it behind him. Leaving her alone to catch her breath, put some stiffeners in her knees and recover what little dignity remained after she'd flung herself at a total stranger.

Okay, there had been some heavy-duty flirting going on, but most of it had been on her side. Dante, realising that she was in a mess, had tried to sit her down and quietly explain about the apartment while she had put on a display that wouldn't have disgraced a burlesque dancer. One minute she'd been struggling with her glove and the next…

Where on earth had that performance come from? She wasn't that woman.

Bad enough, but when he'd told her that she'd been the victim of some Internet con she'd practically thrown herself at him.

What on earth had she been *thinking*?

What on earth must *he* be thinking?

Well, that was easy. He had to be thinking that she'd do anything in return for a bed for the night and who could blame him?

As for her, she hadn't been thinking at all. She might have been telling herself that she was going to grab every moment, live her mother's 'seize the day' philosophy, but it was like learning how to parachute: you had to make practice jumps first—learn how to fall before you leapt out of a plane or the landing was going to be painful.

Cheeks burning, her mouth throbbing with heat, she dampened the corner of the towel he'd used to dry her hand and laid it against her hot face before, legs shaking, she sank down onto the side of the bath.

'Mum,' she whispered, her head on her knees. 'Help...'

CHAPTER THREE

*'Ice cream is cheaper than therapy and you
don't need an appointment.'*

—from *Rosie's Little Book of Ice Cream*

DANTE WALKED INTO the kitchen, filled a glass
with ice-cold water from the fridge and downed
it in one. The only effect was to make him feel
as if he had steam coming out of his ears and,
from the way Lisa was looking at him, he very
well might have.

Angelica...

Her name suggested something white and gold
in a Renaissance painting, but no Renaissance
angel ever had a body, legs like that. A mouth
that felt like a kiss from across the room. A kiss
that obliterated every thought but to possess her.

He hadn't looked at a woman in that way,
touched a woman in that way for over a year but
when he'd turned, seen her crimson mouth, the
one jolt of colour against the unrelieved black of

her clothes, her hair, against skin that looked as if it had never seen the sun, every cell in his body had sat up and begged to go to hell.

Someone must have been listening...

Dark Angel was right.

Aware that Lisa was regarding him with un-disguised amusement, brows raised a fraction, he stared right back at her, daring her to say a word. She grinned knowingly then turned away as Angelica finally joined them.

'How did he do?' Lisa asked. 'Has he earned his first aid badge?'

'Gold star,' Angelica replied, holding out her hand for inspection. She was doing a good job of matching Lisa's jokey tone but she wasn't looking at him and there was a betraying pink flush across her cheekbones.

'Did you find a box, Lis?' he asked sharply.

'I have *this* box,' she said, 'thoroughly lined with newspaper.' She looked down at the deep box she was holding and then up at him, her brows a *got you* millimetre higher and he could have kicked himself. So much for attempting to distract her. 'Chef gave me some minced chicken for Rattino. I assumed you'd have milk up here.'

'I have, but it'll be cold,' he said, grabbing the

excuse to escape. 'I'll put a drop in the micro-wave to take the chill off.'

'Thank you. That's very kind,' Angelica replied quietly as she took the box from Lisa and retreated to the bathroom. He watched her walk away, trying not to think about what her legs were doing to him. What he wanted to do to her legs...

He turned abruptly, opened the fridge door, poured some milk into a saucer and put it in the microwave for a few seconds.

'Haven't you got something to do downstairs?' he asked as, feeling like an idiot with Lisa watching, he put a finger in to test the temperature.

'It's snowing hard now. Everyone's making a move and I've told the staff to go home.' She leaned against the door frame. 'What are you going to do about Geli?'

'Do?'

'If it's true about her apartment.'

'It's true about Via Pepone,' he said. 'My father demolished it last year. He's about to put a glass box in its place.'

'That's the place—?'

'Yes,' he said, cutting her off before she said any more.

'Right.' She waited a moment and then glanced towards the bathroom. 'So?'

'So what?' he snapped.

'So what are you going to do about Geli?'

'Why should I do anything?' he demanded. 'My father may have demolished the street but he didn't con her out of rent for an apartment that no longer exists.' Lisa didn't say anything but her body language was very loud. 'What do you expect me to do, Lis? Pick her up and put her in my pocket like one of her strays? Have we got a cardboard box big enough?'

'No,' she said. 'But she's been travelling all day, it's late and, in case you hadn't noticed, it's snowing out there.'

'I'd noticed.' Snowflakes had been clinging to Angelica's hair and face when she'd arrived. She'd licked one off her upper lip as she'd walked towards him.

'That's it?' Lisa asked. 'That's all you've got?'

'Lis…'

'It's okay; don't worry about it.' She raised a hand in a gesture that was pure Italian. 'I've got a room she can have.'

'A room?'

'Four walls, ceiling, bed—'

'I wasn't asking for a definition,' he said, 'I was questioning the reality. You and Baldacci live in a one-bedroom flat and Angelica's legs would hang over the end of your sofa.' He could picture them. Long legs, short skirt, sexy boots—

'The sofa is a non-starter,' she agreed, 'but the room is here, just along the corridor. Right next to yours.'

That jolted him out of his fantasy. 'That's not your room!'

'No? Whose clothes are hanging in the wardrobe? Whose book is on the bedside table? Nonnina Rosa believes that it's my room and that, my dear cousin, makes it a fact.'

'Nonnina Rosa is on the other side of the world.'

'She's just a second away in cyber space. You wouldn't want her to discover that when I self-lessly volunteered—'

'Selflessly? *Madonna!*'

'—when I selflessly volunteered to come half-way across the world to pick up the pieces and glue you back together, you did nothing to stop me from moving in with a Baldacci?' She mimed her grandmother spitting at the mention of the hated name. 'Would you?'

'The only reason you're here is because Vanni

Baldacci's father sent him to his Milan office to keep him out of the scheming clutches of a Vettori.'

'Epic fail. The darling man has just texted me to say he's on his way with my gumboots and a brolly.'

'Lisa, please...'

'Nonnina was desperately worried about you, Dan. She felt responsible—'

'What happened had nothing to do with her. It was my choice. And you were about as much use as a chocolate teapot,' he added before she could rerun what had happened. It was over, done with. 'The only reason I keep you on is because no one else will employ you.'

She lifted her shoulders in a theatrical shrug. 'Whatever,' she said, not bothering to challenge him. 'Of course, if you object so strongly to Geli having my room you could always invite her to share yours.'

'Go away, Lisa, or I swear I'll call Nonnina myself. Or maybe I should speak to Nicolo Baldacci.'

'How long is it, exactly, since you got laid, Dan?' she asked, not in the least bothered by a threat that they both knew he would never carry out. 'It's time to forget Valentina. You need to get back on the horse.'

He picked up the saucer of milk and waited for her to move.

'I mean it. You've been looking at Geli like a starving man who's been offered hot food ever since she walked through the door,' she said, staying right where she was. 'In fact, if I were a betting woman I'd be offering straight odds that you were taking the first mouthful when I interrupted you.'

'I met her less than an hour ago,' he reminded her, trying not to think about the feel of Angelica's tongue on his lip even as he sucked it in to taste her. Coffee, honey, life…

'An hour can be a lifetime when lightning strikes. I wanted to rip Vanni's clothes off the minute I set eyes on him,' she said with the kind of smile that suggested it hadn't been much longer than that.

'I'm not about to take advantage of a damsel in distress.'

'Not even if she wants you to take advantage of her? She looked…interested.'

'Not even then,' he said, trying not to think about her crimson lips whispering *'caldo...'*, her breath against his mouth, the way she'd leaned into him, how her body fitted against his.

'You are so damned English under that Italian exterior,' she said. 'Always the perfect gentleman. Never betraying so much as a quiver of emotion, even when the damsel in question is stomping all over you in her designer stilettos.'

'Valentina knew what she wanted. I was the one who moved the goalposts.'

'Don't be so damned noble. You fall in love with the man, Dan, not some fancy penthouse, the villa at Lake Como, the A-list lifestyle. I'd live in a cave with Vanni.'

'Then talk to your parents before your secret blows up in your faces.' Dante had experienced that pain at first-hand... 'It won't go away, Lis.'

'No.' She pulled a face, muttered, 'Stupid feud...' Then she reached out and touched his arm. 'I'll leave you to it. Good luck with finding a hotel that'll take Rattino,' she said, heading towards the door. She didn't get more than a couple of steps before she stopped, turned round. 'I suppose Geli could put him back in her coat pocket and sneak him in—'

'Are you done?' he asked, losing patience.

'—but it will only be a temporary solution.

Tonight's scene in the bar will be the talk of the market tomorrow.'

'The snow will be the talk of the market tomorrow.'

She shook her head. 'It snows every year but the combination of a head-turning woman, the rare sound of Dante Vettori laughing and a rat? Now that is something worth talking about.'

'Lis,' he warned.

'Never mind. I'm sure you'll think of something.'

'You don't want to know what I'm thinking.'

She grinned. 'I know exactly what you're thinking. You and every man in the bar when she arrived in a flurry of snowflakes. How to make an entrance! Tra-la-la…' Lisa blew on her fingers and then shook them. 'Seriously, Dan, I don't know if Geli needs a job but she will need space to show her stuff and having her around will be very good for business.'

'Are you done now?'

'As for the other thing, my advice is to get in quickly or you're going to be at the back of a very long queue.' She almost made it to the door before she said, 'You won't forget that you offered her supper? Have you got anything up here or do you want me to look in the fridge?'

'Just lock up and go home.'

'Okay.' She opened the door, looked back over her shoulder. 'I've brought up Geli's suitcase, by the way. It's in her room.'

'Basta! Andare!'

'And you have lipstick—' she pointed to the corner of her own mouth '—just here.'

Geli's hands were shaking as she scooped out a tiny portion of chicken for the kitten, her whole body trembling as she sank to her knees beside the bath, resting her chin on her arms as she watched him practically inhale it. Trying to decide which was most disturbing—kissing a man she'd only just met or being told that the flat she'd paid good money to rent did not exist.

It should be the flat. Obviously.

Elle was going to be furious with her for being so careless. Her grandmother had lost everything but the roof over their heads to a con man not long after their mother died. Without their big sister putting her own life on hold to take care of them all, she and Sorrel would have ended up in care.

Fortunately, there was the width of France and Switzerland between them. Unless she told them what had happened they would never know that she'd messed up.

Which left the kiss. Which was ridiculous. It wasn't as if it was her first kiss—her first any-thing—but for a moment she'd felt as if she'd been on the brink of something rare, something life-changing.

As she leaned against the edge of the bath watching the kitten, she remembered the mo-ment when she'd caught her sister on the point of kissing Sean McElroy. Their closeness, the in-tensity of their focus on each other, had terrified her. Elle was hers—surrogate mother, surrogate father, big sister, carer—but suddenly there was someone else, this man, a total stranger, getting all her attention.

For a moment, with Dante's arm around her waist, his lips a millimetre from her own, she'd known how Elle had felt, had wanted it for her-self. That was why she was shaking. For a mo-ment she had been utterly defenceless…

'I'm sorry I took so long to bring the milk. I was arranging with Lisa to lock up for me.' Dante placed the saucer in the bath but, instead of joining her, he stood back, keeping his distance.

Which was a very good thing, she told herself. Just because she wanted him here, kneeling beside her, didn't make it a good idea...

'We're putting you to a lot of trouble,' she said, keeping her eyes fixed on the kitten as he stepped in the saucer and lapped clumsily at the milk.

'He's looking better already,' he said, his voice as distant as his body.

'He's fluffed up a bit now he's dry but he hasn't learned to wash.' Keep it impersonal. Talk about the cat... 'He's much too young to be separated from his mother. I'll take him back to where I found him tomorrow and see if I can reunite them.'

'How do you think that will work out?' he asked.

'About as well as it usually does.' She reached out and ran a finger over the kitten's tiny domed head. 'About as well as my escape to Isola is working out.'

'Escape? What are you running away from?'

She looked up. He was frowning, evidently concerned. 'Just life in a small village,' she said quickly before he began wondering which asylum she'd broken out of. 'Conformity. I very nearly succumbed to the temptation to buckle down to reality and become the design director for my sisters' ice cream parlour franchise.' She did a little mock shiver. 'Can you *imagine*? All that *pink*!'

He snorted with laughter.

'You see? You only met me half an hour ago but even you can see that's ridiculous.'

'Let's just say that I find it unlikely.'

'Thank you, Dante. You couldn't have paid me a nicer compliment.' She hooked her hair behind her ear, stood up and faced him. *Forget the kiss...* 'And thank you for trying to break the news about my apartment gently over supper.'

He shrugged. 'I wanted more information before I leapt in with the bad news,' he said, turning away to reach for a towel. 'You could have made a mistake with the address.'

'But you didn't believe I had.'

'No.' He stopped looking down at the towel and looked at her. 'The map you had was out of date. If you had followed the directions you were given, you would have ended up at a construction site.'

'Which I did,' she admitted. 'Lisa was right

when she said you know Isola like the back of your hand.'

'I spent a lot of my childhood here but it's changing fast. We're struggling to hang on to what's left.'

'You'll forgive me if I say that I wish you'd struggled a little harder.' He didn't exactly flinch but clearly she'd said the wrong thing. 'I'm sorry. It's not your fault.'

'Here, Rattino will be more comfortable on this,' he said. 'Bring the box through to the fire when he's settled.'

She looked down at the towel he'd thrust into her hand and then at the space where, a moment before, Dante Vettori had been standing.

What had she said?

Everything about Dante was still except the hand holding the wooden spoon as he stirred something in a saucepan. The light glinting off the heavy steel band of his wristwatch was mesmerising and Geli could have stood in the doorway and watched him for ever.

'Is he settled?' he asked without looking up.

'Asleep and dreaming he's in heaven,' she said. 'Life is so simple when you're a cat.' She held up the lease that was currently severely complicating hers.

He turned down the heat and took it from her. 'There's no mistake about the address,' he said.

'No. I have Signora Franco's number,' she said, clutching the phone she'd used to tell her sisters that she'd arrived safely. Well, she'd arrived... 'If I call her will you talk to her?'

'Of course.'

The wait to connect seemed endless but, in the end, was nowhere near long enough.

'No reply?' he asked when she let the phone drop to her side.

She shook her head. 'The message was in Italian, but "number unavailable" sounds the same in any language.'

He shook his head. 'Tell me, Angelica, how did you learn such impressive self-control?'

She held her breath momentarily. Let it out slowly. 'Self-control?'

'Few women I know—few men, come to that— would have taken the news about the apartment without throwing something, even if it was just a tantrum.'

'Oh...' Momentarily thrown, she said, 'I don't do tantrums.'

'Is there a secret to that? Anything you're prepared to share with Lisa?' he asked.

'Yoga?' she offered. 'It's all in the breathing.'

He turned back to the sauce without a word, stirring it very slowly.

Damn it, she didn't know him... He might regret kissing her but he'd been kind when he didn't have to be. He hadn't yelled at her, or thrown her or the kitten out when they'd caused a near riot in his café.

She took one of those yoga breaths.

'I cried a lot when my mother died. It made things difficult at school and my sisters sad because there was nothing they could do to make things better.' This was something she never talked about and the words escaped in a soft rush of breath. 'I wanted to stop but I didn't know how.'

'How old were you?' He continued to stir the sauce, not looking at her.

'Eight.' Two days short of her ninth birthday.

'Eight?' He swung round. *Madre de Dio...*'

'It was cancer,' she said before he asked. 'The aggressive kind, where the diagnosis comes with weeks to live.'

'*Non c'è niente che posso dire,*' he said. And then, in English, 'There are no words...'

'No.' She shook her head. 'There's nothing anyone can say. No words, not an entire river of tears... Nothing can change what happened.'

'Is that when you stopped crying?' he asked. 'When you realised it made no difference?'

'I was eight, Dante!' So much for her self-control...

'So?' he prompted, 'you were too young for philosophy but clearly something happened.'

'What? Oh, yes... My grandmother found an old black hat in the attic. With a floppy brim,' she said, describing in with a wavy gesture. 'Crocheted. Very Sixties. My grandmother was something of a style icon in her day.'

'And that helped?' he asked, ignoring the fashion note that was meant to draw a thick black line under the subject.

'She said that when I was sad I could hide behind the brim.' She still remembered the moment she'd put it on. The feeling of a great burden being lifted from her shoulders. 'It showed the world what I was feeling without the red eyes and snot and was a lot easier for everyone to live with. I wore that hat until it fell apart.'

'And then what did you do?'

'I found a black cloche in a charity shop. And a black dress. It was too big for me but my grandmother helped me cut it down. Then, when I was twelve, I dyed my hair.'

'Let me guess. Black.'

'Actually, it was nearer green but my grandmother took me to the hairdressers' and had it sorted out and dyed properly.' The memory of the moment when she'd looked in the mirror and seen herself still made her smile. 'My sisters were furious.'

'Because of the colour or because they hadn't had the same treat?'

'Because Grandma had blown all the housekeeping money on rescuing me from the nightmare of going to school with green hair. They thought eating was more important.'

'Hunger has a tendency to shorten the temper,' he agreed, turning the sauce down to minimum and pouring two glasses of wine from a bottle, dewed with moisture, that stood on the china-laden dresser that took up most of one wall.

'Where was your father in all this?' he asked as he handed a glass to her.

'I don't have one. None of us do.'

His eyebrows rose a fraction. 'Unless there's been a major leap forward in evolution that passed me by,' he said, leaning back against the dresser, 'that's not possible.'

'Biologically perhaps, but while my mother loved babies, she didn't want a man underfoot, being moody when his dinner wasn't ready.' She turned and, glass in hand, leaned back against the dresser. It was easier being beside him than looking at him. 'My grandparents' marriage was not a happy one.' She took a mouthful of the rich, fruity wine. 'I imagine the first time she got pregnant it was an accident, but after that, whenever she was broody, she helped herself to a sperm donation from some man she took a fancy to. A travelling fair visits the village every year for the Late Spring Bank Holiday,' she said. 'Our fathers were setting up in the next county before the egg divided.'

'She lived dangerously.'

'She lived for the moment.'

'"Take what you want," says God, "take it and pay for it..."' He glanced sideways at her. 'It's an old Spanish proverb. So? What colour is your hair?'

She picked up a strand, looked at it, then up at him. 'Black.'

He grinned and it wasn't just the wine that was warming her.

'How did you find it?' he asked. 'The apartment.'

'What? Oh…' Well, that was short-lived… 'On the internet.' He didn't have to say what he thought about that. A muscle tightening at the corner of his mouth wrote an entire essay on the subject. 'It was an international agency,' she protested, 'affiliated to goodness knows how many associations.' Not that she'd checked on any of them. Who did? 'There were comments from previous tenants. Some who'd enjoyed their stay in the apartment and couldn't wait to come back, and a few disgruntled remarks about the heat and the lack of air conditioning. Exactly what you'd expect. Look, I'll show you,' she said, clicking the link on her smartphone.

Like the phone line, the web link was no longer available.

Until that moment she hadn't believed that she'd been conned, had been sure that it was all a mistake, but now the air was sucked right out of her and Dante caught her as her knees buckled, rescued her glass, turned her into his chest.

His arm was around her, her head against his shoulder and the temptation to stay there and allow him to hold her, comfort her, almost overwhelmed her. It felt so right, he was such a perfect fit, but she'd already made a fool of herself once today. She dragged in a deep breath, straightened her shoulders and stepped away.

'Are you okay?' he said, his hand still outstretched to steady her.

'Fine. Really.'

He didn't look convinced. 'When did you last have something to eat?'

'I don't know. I had a sandwich at the airport when they announced that my flight had been delayed.'

'Nothing since then?' He looked horrified. 'No wonder you're trembling. Sit down while the pasta cooks.' He tested it. 'Another minute or two. It's nothing fancy—*pasta al funghi*. Pasta with mushroom sauce,' he added in case her Italian wasn't up to it.

She shook her head. 'I'm sure it's wonderful but, honestly, I couldn't eat a thing.' He didn't argue but reached for a couple of dishes. 'The apartment looked so perfect and the rent was so reasonable…' *Stupid, stupid, stupid!* 'I assumed it was because it was the middle of winter, off-season, but it was a trap for the gullible. No, make that the cheap.' She'd had it hammered into her by Elle that if something looked too good… But she'd been enchanted.

'Did you give them details of your bank account?' Dante asked.

'What? No… At least…I set up a direct debit for the rent…' As she realised what he was getting at, she blinked, looked down at her phone and then swiftly keyed in her password.

As she saw the balance she felt the blood leave her head.

CHAPTER FOUR

'When things are bad, send ice cream. With hot fudge sauce, sprinkles and mini-marsh-mallows.'

—from *Rosie's Little Book of Ice Cream*

'MADONNA...'

Dante caught her before she hit the floor and carried her through to the living room. He placed her gently on the sofa, her head flat and her feet propped up on the arm, and knelt beside her until she opened her eyes.

For a moment they were blank as she tried to work out what had happened, where she was.

'Angelica...' She blinked, focused, saw him, tried to sit up but he put a hand on her shoulder. 'Lie still for a moment. Breathe...'

He'd thought she was pale before but now she was white, emphasising the size of those extraordinary silver fox eyes, the splendour of her luscious crimson mouth.

'What happened?'

'You fainted.'

She groaned. 'How unutterably pathetic.'

'The combination of shock and a lack of food,' he suggested. Then, as she made an effort to sit up, 'No. Stay there. I'll get you some water.'

'Dante—' For a moment she challenged him, but then sank back against the cushion. 'Why do you call me Angelica?'

'Geli is not a name for a grown woman.'

'Oh…' She thought about it for a moment. 'Right.'

Once he was sure that she was going to stay put, he fetched a glass of water from the kitchen. Angelica had dropped her phone and, as he bent to pick it up, he saw why she'd fainted. The con artists had cleaned her out.

He half expected her to be sitting up, fretting when he returned but she was exactly where he'd left her, flat on her back but with one arm thrown across her eyes. The gesture had pulled up her dress, exposing even more of her thighs, and it was a toss-up whether he gave her the water or threw it over himself.

'Here,' he said, 'take a sip of this.'

She removed her arm, turned her head to look

up at him. 'Your first aid skills are being thoroughly tested this evening.'

'I may have been a bit slow on the kissing-it-better cure,' he assured her, 'but I remembered the head down, feet up recovery position for a faint.'

'Gold star. I said so...' She made a move to sit up and take the glass.

'Don't sit up too quickly,' he said, slipping his arm beneath her shoulders to support her while he held it to her lips.

'Sì, dottore...' She managed a smile which, under the circumstances, was pretty brave but drew unnecessary attention to her mouth. The temptation to see just how much kissing it would take to make this better was almost irresistible. So much for his declaration to Lisa about not taking advantage...

Putting the glass down on the end table, he moved to the safety of her feet.

'What are you doing?' she asked when he slid a hand beneath her ankle and reached for the zip of her boot.

'Taking off your boots. Didn't they teach you that at your very comprehensive first aid course?'

'Absolutely. It came right after kissing it better, but I thought you were absent that day.'

'It's just common sense. Everyone feels better with their boots off.'

'That's true,' she said, stretching her foot and wiggling her long toes. Apparently there was no 'safe end' when it came to Angelica Amery, and he quickly dispensed with the second boot and took a step away.

'Okay. You can sit up when you feel up to it,' he said, 'but slowly. Take your time.'

She eased herself up into the corner of the sofa, smoothing her skirt down and tucking her feet beneath her. 'What happened to my phone, Dante? I have to call the bank.'

He took it from his pocket and handed it to her.

'You saw?' she asked.

'When I picked it up. Will they refund you?'

She sighed. 'Not the first month's rent and deposit, that's for sure. I created the direct debit so that was a legitimate withdrawal as far as they're concerned. The rest would appear to be straightforward fraud so I should get that back. Eventually.' She found the number in her contact list and hit call. 'After they've done everything in their power to imply that it's my fault.' She looked up at him. 'Dante...'

'Angelica?'

'Thank you. For catching me.'

'Any time.'

The jet brooch at her throat moved as she swallowed down her emotions. 'You rate a gold star while I'm a triple chocolate idiot. With fudge topping. And sprinkles.'

'You won't be the only one who's been caught.'

'That doesn't make me feel any less stupid.' She shook her head then winced, clearly wishing she hadn't, and he had a hand out to comfort her before he could stop himself. Fortunately, she was listening to the prompts and didn't see. 'I should have run some checks, but we'd found a short-term tenant for the house and it was all a bit of a rush.'

'You've let your home in England?'

'Yes.' So, even if she wanted to, she couldn't run for home... 'My sisters moved out when they married so it was just me, Grandma and Great-Uncle Basil. Grandma's arthritis was playing up and Basil wanted to take her somewhere warm for the winter so we decided to let the house to finance it—'

'And you were in a rush to escape from the horror of all that pink and white ice cream.'

'I shouldn't mock it.' She managed a somewhat watery smile. 'Ice cream has been very good to my family and, let's face it, art and fashion have never been safe career choices.'

'We do what we have to.'

'Yes...'

Leaving her to speak to the bank, he returned to the kitchen. She might think she had no appetite, but if it was put in front of her it was possible that she would be tempted.

When he returned, with a tray containing two bowls of *pasta al funghi*, a couple of forks and some napkins, she was staring into the fire.

'Sorted?' he asked, and she surprised him with a grin. 'What?'

'*"Sorted..."* You sound so Italian and yet you use English as if it was your first language. It sounds odd.'

'Not that odd. My mother is English.'

'That has to help,' she said.

'That and the fact that when she left my father she took me with her to England and refused to speak another word of Italian for as long as she lives.'

'Tough on you.'

He shrugged but there was nothing like a reminder of that first endless cold, wet English summer hearing, speaking only an alien language, to dampen his libido.

Her eyes softened. 'How old were you?'

He handed her a fork, wishing he'd kept his mouth shut. 'Twelve, just coming up to my thirteenth birthday.'

'A bad age.'

'Is there a good one?'

She shook her head. 'I guess not, but it was tough enough to be faced with your parents splitting up without losing your home, your language.'

'My mother was angry, hurt...' He shrugged. 'She'd discovered that my father had been having an affair with the woman she thought was her best friend. She offered me the choice to go with her or to stay in Italy.'

'And you chose her.'

'She needed me more than he did.' He passed her a bowl of pasta. 'Eat...'

She looked at the dish she was holding as if unsure how it had got there but, as he'd hoped, she was too well-mannered not to eat food put in front of her. 'It smells very good,' she said politely and took a mouthful.

'Life is short,' he said as he settled at the far end of the sofa. 'Eat pasta every day.'

'I have to admit that on a cold, snowy Milan night it's the perfect comfort food.' Her brave attempt at a smile lit up her eyes, fringed with thick lashes and set in a soft smudge of charcoal. It went straight to his groin and he propped his foot on one knee in an attempt to keep that fact to himself. The kiss had been a mistake. Kissing anyone was a mistake... 'Of course, come spring I might be persuaded to make you a Bellini sorbet and then it would be a close run thing,' she added.

'A Bellini sorbet?' he repeated, mentally grabbing onto the thought of something ice-cold slipping down his throat.

'Fresh peach juice, Prosecco... The real thing, sparkling on the tongue, but frozen.' She raised her eyebrows. 'Oh, I see. You thought my sisters use mass-produced vegetable fat goo for their events business.'

He shrugged. 'The British are not famous for their ice cream.'

'Unlike Italians?'

'I believe you mentioned an ice cream van? If it's one of those stop-me-and-buy-one vans it won't be loaded up with Bellini sorbet.'

'True, but Rosie is a bit special. She goes to children's parties, hen nights, weddings…any fun bash that ice cream is going to enhance.'

'Is there a demand for that?'

'Huge. Of course, the fact that she makes the occasional appearance in a popular television soap opera means that we could book her three times over. We…they…my sisters…also make bespoke ices for weddings, corporate events and the like—that's the Bellini sorbet market—and now Sorrel, she's the sister with the business brain, is franchising a chain of retro American-style ice cream parlours.'

'And you design the interiors?'

With luck, talking would keep her mind off the non-existent flat until she'd finished the pasta. He prompted her to talk about how the business had evolved, looked at the photographs on her phone of the ice cream parlours she'd designed. She was very talented…

'So, you're a designer, an ice cream maker and you rescue kittens in your spare time?' he asked.

'Rescue is a two-way thing, Dante. People think

that cats are selfish, but I've seen them respond to need in their owners and in other animals.'

As she looked up at him from under those heavy lashes he found himself wondering who, in the kitten scenario, was rescuing whom. He sensed something deeper than a desire to paint, design, experience Italy behind her 'escape', but they were already way too deep into personal territory; he had no wish to hear more.

Maybe she sensed it too because she took another mouthful of the pasta. 'This is really good.'

'Wait until you try chef's *Risotto alla Milanese*. Arborio rice from the Po Valley, butter, dry white wine, saffron and Parmigiano-Reggiano.' Food was always a safe topic. 'I'm sorry you missed it but, with the weather closing in, Lisa sent everyone home.'

'Now that is really impressive.'

'Sending staff home early on a bad night?'

She shook her head, then said, 'Well, yes, but I was referring to your ability to name the ingredients in the risotto recipe.'

He shrugged. 'Nonnina used to make it for me,' he said.

'Nonnina? That's your grandmother, right?'

'Actually, she's Lisa's grandmother, my great-aunt, but everyone calls her Nonnina,' he said. 'Café Rosa was her bar until she finally surrendered to pressure from her son to retire and join him and his family in Australia. She used to let me help in the kitchen when I was a boy.'

She smiled. 'That's a sweet picture, but I think you were wise not to step into her shoes and take over the cooking.'

'Oh? And why is that?'

'You forgot the chicken stock.'

'Did I?' He sensed a subtext, something he was missing. 'Does it matter?'

'It does if you're the chicken.'

'Don't tell me,' he said, 'you find them wandering, lost or abandoned, and put them in your pocket—no, in the basket of your bicycle. Do you put them in the bath, too?'

She grinned. 'I wouldn't advise you to try that with a chicken. They can't fly, but they do a very energetic flap and a panicky bird in a confined space is going to make a heck of a mess.'

'You are a fount of wisdom on the animal welfare front. So, what do you do with them?' he asked. 'Should the occasion ever arise.'

'I take injured birds to the local animal sanctuary, to be cared for until they can be released or found a good home.'

'Not to the vet?'

She tilted her head in an awkward little movement. 'I found a pheasant once. It had been winged by a shotgun and had taken cover in our hedge. I picked it up and carried it across the village to the vet, expecting him to take care of it. He didn't even bother to look at it, just wrung its neck, handed it back to me and told me to make sure my mother hung it for a few days before she cooked it.'

'*Perdio!* How old were you?'

'Nine.' She sketched a shrug. 'Grandma and I gave the poor thing a very elaborate funeral and buried it in the garden.'

'I hope your grandmother tore a strip off the vet.'

'No. She told me that he was an old school farm vet who thought he was giving a useful life lesson to a girl who lived in the country. No sentiment there.' She stirred the pasta with her fork. 'At least he was honest. He could have sent me on my way, promising to take care of the bird, and then eaten it himself.'

With his head now filled with the picture of a

motherless little girl clutching a dead pheasant, he really wished he hadn't asked. And then her comment about the chicken stock registered. 'Are you a vegetarian, Angelica?'

'I don't eat meat,' she said.

'Is there a difference?'

'I don't wear fur, but I wear leather and wool and use it in my clothes. I don't eat meat, but I eat fish and cheese and eggs and I pour milk over my cereals.' She circled her fork over the dish she was holding to prove her point. 'I am fully aware of the hypocrisy.'

'I think you're being a little hard on yourself,' he said. 'Why didn't you say something earlier? When I ordered the risotto for you?'

'I was about to when events overtook us and actually this is perfect. One of my favourites,' she said, making an effort to eat a little more. 'Is it a problem for you?'

'Of course not; why would it be? It's just I'm surprised, that's all.'

She raised an eyebrow. 'Surprised? Why?'

'You are aware that you dress like a vampire?'

'Oh *that*,' she said, the corner of her mouth twitching into a smile. 'That's what Sean called me, the first time he set eyes on me. A skinny vampire.'

Sean? Who was Sean? Don't ask... 'That must have been some time ago,' he said.

'I was sixteen. I've put on a bit of weight since then,' she said, looking down at the soft curves of her breasts and then up at him and caught him doing the same.

For a moment nothing seemed to move and in his head, above the drumming of his heartbeat, he could hear Lisa asking how long it had been since he'd been laid.

Until tonight he hadn't noticed, hadn't cared, but then Angelica Amery had walked into his bar and it was as if she'd hit the start button on the part of him that, for self-protection, he'd switched off months ago. The part that could rage, react, *feel*. The moment he'd turned, seen her sparkling with snow, he'd known that all he had to do was put out his hand, touch her, and the life would come flooding back. And, like blood returning to a numb limb, the pain would follow.

He'd spent the last months concentrating on work, using it to create an impermeable membrane between his public life—devoting himself to this community, *his* community—and the vacuum within.

In a vacuum no one could hear you scream...

'Who's Sean?' he asked. She frowned at his abruptness. 'You said Sean called you a skinny vampire.'

'Oh, right. He's my brother-in-law,' she said. 'He and Elle have three little girls.' Her smile was something else, lighting up her face, making him want to smile right back. 'As for the vampire thing, it's just a look, Dante. I don't bite. Well, not often.' She scooped up another forkful of pasta. 'Just a little nip here, a little nip there but, unlike the kitten, I make it a rule to never draw blood.'

'A pity. I suspect that having you kiss it better would be an unforgettable experience.' Then, before she could speak, 'I'm sorry, that was—'

'No. I'm the one who has to apologise.' The pasta never made it to her mouth. 'I don't normally fling myself at total strangers.' She gave up pretending to eat and put down her fork. 'What am I saying? I *never* fling myself at total strangers. It must have been the shock—'

'Don't!' Without thinking, he'd reached out and put his hand over hers to stop her and the pulse in the tip of his thumb began to pick up speed, thrum in his ears. His brain did a desperate drive-by of all the meaningless phrases one used to cover awkward moments. None fitted. 'Don't apologise.' He didn't want her to apologise for kissing him so he said the only thing in his head—the truth. 'It's quite the best thing that's happened to me in a while.'

And that rushing in his ears had to be the sound of life pouring through the gaping hole she'd punched through his impermeable membrane.

Removing his hand, he abandoned his own supper and then, because he had to do something, he got up and opened the doors of the wood burner. 'What did the bank say?' he asked as he tossed in a couple of logs.

She didn't answer and he half turned.

'They took the details,' she said quickly. 'Asked me a load of questions. I got the feeling they thought, or maybe just hoped, that I'd shared my password with a boyfriend who'd done the dirty and cleaned me out.'

'It happens.'

'Not to me!' Perhaps realising that she'd used rather more vehemence than necessary, she said, 'My grandmother lost everything to a con artist not long after my mother died. He was elegant, charming, endlessly patient with us girls. He even bought me some black hair ribbons. It wasn't just Grandma. We all fell for him, even the dog. It took us a long time to recover. Financially and emotionally.'

'Is that why you're so angry with yourself?' he asked, standing up. 'You shouldn't be. You're as much a victim as if you'd been mugged in the street.'

'I know, but damn it, Dante, it was just so *perfect*. The living room had French windows that opened onto a tiny balcony with a distant view of the Duomo and there was a small second bedroom that I was going to use as a workroom...' She shook her head. 'I'm sorry. I know it doesn't exist but I'm still having trouble getting my head around this.'

'You know what's happened, but it's taking some parts of your brain a while to catch up.'

He knew how it was. He still had sleepless night reruns of the day he'd laid everything out for Valentina, giving her the choice to stay or walk away. She'd used everything she had—soft words and scorching sex—in a last-ditch effort to persuade him to change his mind. Trying to rewrite the scene, behaved better. She pulled a face. 'I guess.'

'A delayed flight, bad weather and then discovering that you're a victim of fraud would be enough to cloud anyone's thoughts.'

'Mine appear to be denser than mud.'

'Have you any idea what you will do?' he asked. 'Stay or go home?'

She lifted her shoulders. 'If I go home I'll be in the same situation as if I stay. Nowhere to live, no job, no money until the bank sorts out a refund. *If* the bank sorts out a refund.'

'What about your sisters?'

'Oh, they'd give me a room and a job like a shot but then I'll be stepping back into the role of baby sister. A big black cuckoo in the happy families' nest.' She glanced at her watch. 'It's late. Is there a B&B close by? A *pensione*? Somewhere that would take me in at this time of night?'

'Close enough.' He turned back to the fire and gave it a prod with the poker, sending up a cloud of sparks. 'Lisa has given you her room. It's the one opposite the bathroom.'

'Bathroom?' She frowned as she tried to make sense of that. 'Do you mean her room here? In this apartment? But I couldn't possibly—'

'There's a lock on the door,' he said before she could finish.

'What? No…' He couldn't be sure whether she had blushed or it was the glow from the fire warming her cheeks. 'I meant I couldn't possibly impose on you.'

'I think you should try,' he said. 'As you said, it's late and there's the additional problem—'

'I have some cash. And a credit card for use in emergencies. I'd say this counts as an emergency, wouldn't you?'

'Undoubtedly, but if you'd let me finish? I was going to say that there's a problem with the kitten. He's not going to find much of a welcome in a hotel.'

'I could—'

'No,' he said. 'You couldn't.'

'You don't know what I was going to say.'

'You were going to say that you could put him back in your pocket and no one would ever know.' He raised an eyebrow, daring her to deny it. 'We all know how that turned out this evening.'

'Okay, so the kitten is a problem,' she admitted, 'but what about Lisa?'

'What about her?'

'If I have her room, where will she sleep?'

'Where she always sleeps,' he said. 'She keeps a few things here just in case there's an unannounced visit from her family, but she actually lives with Giovanni.'

'Really?'

'You think she's a bit old to be worrying what her parents think about her living with her boyfriend?'

'Well, yes.'

Dante had avoided looking at Angelica when he'd told her about the room. Forget the kitten, there was no way he was letting her leave after fainting so dramatically, but the flash of heat between them had complicated what should have been a simple offer of hospitality. She had to believe that there were no strings attached. No expectation that she follow through on a kiss that had fall-into-bed written all over it from the first touch.

He really had to stop thinking about that kiss.

'It's complicated.'

'I can do complicated,' she said. 'I have a very complicated family.'

'True.' He wanted to know all about them. All about her. Almost as much as he didn't... 'But nowhere near as complicated as a hundred-year-old family feud over a goat.'

'A goat?' Angelica looked startled, those hot crimson lips ready to laugh. If she laughed...

'Have you ever taken home a stray goat, Angelica?'

'Oh, please. Even I know that a goat in a well-tended garden is a recipe for disaster. They are particularly partial to roses and my grandmother loves her roses.'

'Goats will eat anything, but it's a story for late at night after good food and too much wine,' he said.

'Mine too,' Angelica said. 'Maybe we should save them for another night?'

'It's a date...'

No. Not a date...

Madonna, this was difficult.

One minute they'd been on the point of ripping one another's clothes off and maybe, just maybe, if he hadn't had time to think, it would have been all right. Now—thanks to an internet con and a stray kitten —Angelica might as well have a 'Do Not Touch' sign around her neck.

'You must be tired. I'll show you the room.'

'Yes... No...' The lace at her throat moved as

she swallowed, the light catching the facets of the jet brooch. 'You and Lisa have both been incredibly kind but you don't know anything about me.' Then, and rather more to the point if she was going to be his roommate for the night, 'I don't know anything about you.'

CHAPTER FIVE

'Eat spinach tomorrow; today is for ice cream.'
—from *Rosie's Little Book of Ice Cream*

'THAT'S NOT TRUE,' Dante said quickly. Too quickly. 'At least not the first part. I've learned a lot about you.' He shut the doors of the wood burner, carefully replaced the poker on its stand and propped his elbow on the mantelpiece, hoping that he looked a lot more relaxed about this than he felt. 'You're a talented designer. You have a wide knowledge of first aid. And ice cream. And you have a complicated family who you care deeply about.' It was there in her voice every time she mentioned them.

'That's not much to go on when you're opening your home to a total stranger.'

'Maybe not, but you're compassionate.' She had also turned every head when she'd walked into his bar—always a bonus—and was the first woman to make him feel like a man in over a year. He should focus on the compassion. 'Despite the fact that you were lost and it was beginning to snow, you still chose to rescue a helpless kitten. I am simply doing—'

'I am not helpless!' Geli said, shifting from calm to heat in a heartbeat, which brought a touch of colour to highlight those fine cheekbones.

'—doing my best to aid a damsel in distress,' he continued, rapidly editing out any reference to helpless or maiden. She was not helpless and no maiden kissed the way she had kissed him.

His reward was a snort of laughter, quickly suppressed. Whether it was at the thought of herself as a damsel or him as a knight errant, he had no way of knowing, but he was glad to have made her laugh, if only briefly.

'Sorry, Dante, but I don't believe in fairy tales.'

'No? All those orphans? All that abuse, abandonment, fear? What's not to believe?' he asked. 'You've just had a very close encounter with the hot breath of the wolf in disguise.'

'Nothing as beautiful as a wolf. Just the cold, unfeeling click of a mouse.' She straightened her back, sat a little taller. 'Okay, I've lost money that I worked hard for, but I'm not going to starve and I'm not going to be sleeping in a shop doorway.'

'Not tonight. And not while there's a room here.'

'I—'

'Tomorrow I'll take you to the *commissariato* so that you can report the fraud,' he said, hoping to distract her. 'You'll need some help with the language.'

'Is there any point? Catching Internet crooks is like trying to catch flies with chopsticks.'

'Made all the harder by the fact that those who've been caught often feel too foolish to report the crime. As if they are in some way to blame for their own misfortune. They're not. You're not,' he said, taking the half-eaten pasta from her.

The colour in her cheeks darkened. 'I know, but I was careless, forgot the basic rule and let my guard down. It will be tougher now to do what I planned, but I am not going to allow a low-life scumbag to steal my dreams and creep home with my tail between my legs.' She took a breath. 'I will not be a victim.'

Her words were heartfelt, passionate, and everything Italian in him wanted to cry out *Bravissima*, kiss her cheeks, wrap her in a warm embrace. His English genes knew better. She wasn't just angry with the criminals; she was angry with herself for falling for the con.

'Basic rule?' he asked.

'Always be suspicious of perfection. If it looks too good to be true, then it almost certainly is.'

'We fall for that one all the time, Angelica. The entire advertising industry is built on that premise. You were meant to fall in love with the apartment and it won't just have been you.'

She sighed. 'No. And it won't just be that apartment, will it? There'll be a host of perfect apartments and villas lined up for the unwary.'

'Undoubtedly. It's your public duty to warn the police that they are likely to be inundated with angry tourists who've paid good money for non-existent accommodation this summer. And maybe stop more people being caught.'

'I suppose...' She tilted her head a little. 'I read somewhere that in Milan the policewomen wear high heels. Is that true?'

'There's only one way to find out,' he said. 'Is it a date?'

'Another one? At this rate we'll be going steady...' Their eyes met and for a moment the air sizzled between them and he was the one swallowing hard. 'It's a date,' she said quickly.

'Can I offer you something else?' he asked. 'Tea, coffee, or do you want to go downstairs and raid the fridge for dessert?'

'Tea?' she repeated, grabbing onto something sane, something sensible. 'Proper tea?'

'Proper tea,' he confirmed.

'Well, now you're talking,' she said, uncurling herself from the corner of the sofa.

'What are you doing?' he asked as she gathered the dishes.

'Whoever cooks in our house is let off the washing-up,' she said, heading for the kitchen before he could tell her to sit down.

'It's a good system,' he said, 'but I do have a dishwasher.'

'You do?'

She looked around and her scepticism was understandable. Apart from the American retro-style fridge he'd installed when he moved in, the kitchen was pretty much as Nonnina had left it. A dresser, loaded with old plates, took up most of one wall, while a family-sized table dominated the centre and a couple of old armchairs stood by the wood stove in the corner—much used in the days when they could only afford to heat one room in winter and the main room was kept for best. It was comfortable, familiar and he liked it the way it was. Which didn't mean he was averse to modern domestic convenience.

'The twenty-first century is through here,' he said, opening the door into what had once been a large pantry but was now a fully fitted utility room. *'Il bagno di servizio.'*

'Magic! You have the best of both worlds.'

'I'm glad you approve.'

Valentina hadn't been impressed, but then his father had given her a personal tour of his apartment in the Quadrilatero d'Oro. He put the kettle on for tea while Angelica stacked the dishes in the machine. The light gleamed on glossy black hair that swung silkily about her shoulders as she moved. On the soft curve of her crimson lips as she turned and saw him watching her.

'It's snowing heavily now,' she said, looking out of the window. 'Will it last?'

'It could be gone by morning, or it could be set in for days,' he said, but he wasn't looking at the snow piling up in the corners of the window. He was looking at her reflection. 'Whichever it is, there's nothing we can do about it.'

'Except enjoy it. If my mother were alive she'd go out and make a snowman.'

'Now?'

'Absolutely. It might turn to rain in the night and the moment would be lost.' The thought brought a smile to her lips. 'She got us all up in the middle of night once, when it had begun to snow. We made snowmen, had a snowball fight and afterwards she heated up tins of tomato soup to warm us up.'

'And was it all gone in the morning?'

'No, but we had a head start on all the other kids.' Her eyes were shining at the memory as she turned to him. 'She never let the chance for fun pass. Maybe she sensed that time was short and she had to make memories for us while she could.'

'Is that what you're doing? Following her example,' he added when she frowned.

'Always say goodbye as if it's for the last time. Live each day as if it's our last...'

'Are you saying that you want to go out and have a snowball fight?' he asked, not wanting to remember how he'd parted from his father.

'Would you come?' she asked but, before he could answer, she shook her head. 'Just kidding. It's been a long day.'

'And you've had a bad introduction to life in

Isola,' he said, although, on reflection, it wasn't an evening which, given the option, he would have missed. 'On the other hand, a little excitement to raise the heartbeat is never a bad thing and you did say that you came to Italy for experience?'

As their eyes met in the reflection in the window he wanted to rewind the clock, stop it at the moment her tongue had touched his lip... Then, as if it was too intimate, intense, she turned to look directly at him.

'Believe me,' she said, catching a yawn, 'it has delivered and then some.'

'You're tired.' She had neither accepted nor refused Lisa's room but, whatever doubts she might have had about staying, whatever doubts he might have about the wisdom of offering it to her, the weather had made the decision for them both. 'Lisa brought up your case,' he said, picking up the mug of tea he'd made her and leading the way to the room his cousin had dressed to make it look, to the casual glance, as if she was using it.

There was a basket of cosmetics on the dressing table, a book beside the bed. A pair of shoes beneath it, lying as if they'd just been kicked off.

'How long has she been living with Giovanni?'

'She followed him here from Melbourne just over a year ago,' he said, picking up Lisa's shoes and tossing them into the wardrobe. 'To be honest, I didn't think their relationship would survive the day-to-day irritations of living together.' Not that he'd cared one way or the other at the time.

'Is that the voice of experience?' she asked.

'I came close once.' He looked at her and she shook her head.

'Not even close,' she said.

'The village gossips?'

'They wouldn't have stopped me.'

'No…' He crossed to the shutters, stood for a moment looking down at the piazza. The snow was blanketing the city in silence, softening the edges, making everything look clean.

Angelica pressed her hands against the window and sighed. 'I love snow.' Her voice was as soft as one of the huge snowflakes sticking to the window and, unable to help himself, he turned and looked at her. 'It's like being in another world,' she said, 'in a place where time doesn't count.' And then she turned from the window and looked up at him.

Geli could feel Dante's warmth as they stood, not quite touching, in front of the cold window.

Everything about the moment was heightened, her senses animal sharp; she could almost hear the thud of his pulse beating a counterpoint to her own, almost taste the pheromones clouding the air. She wanted to tug his shirt from his waistband and rub her cheek against his chest, scent marking him, catlike, as hers.

Lifting his hand in what felt like slow motion, Dante leaned in to her. Her skin tingled, anticipating his touch. Her lips throbbed, hot, feeling twice their normal size. The down on her cheek stirred, lifting to the heat of his hand, and she closed her eyes but his touch never came. Instead, there was the click as he reached over her head to pull shut one of the shutters and every cell in her body screamed *Noooo!*

'My room has an en suite, so the bathroom is all yours,' he said abruptly. 'There's plenty of hot water and no one will disturb you if want to soak off the day.'

No one would disturb her? Was he crazy? She was disturbed beyond reason.

She had nowhere to live, she'd lost her money but all she'd been thinking about was kissing Dante Vettori, ripping open the buttons of his shirt and exploring his warm skin. Imagining how his long fingers would feel curved around her breast—

Click went the second shutter and, released from the mesmerising drift of the snow, she was jolted back to reality and somehow managed a hoarse, 'Thank you.'

He nodded. 'If you need me for anything I'll be downstairs in the office, catching up with the paperwork.'

'I've been keeping you from your work?'

'I'd stopped to eat. That's why I was in the bar when you arrived. You know where everything is. Please…make yourself at home.'

'Dante…' He waited, hand on the door. 'Thank you.'

He responded with the briefest of nods. 'I'll see you in the morning.'

Geli didn't move until she heard the door to the flat close and then her shoulders slumped. How on earth had they come from the promise of a searing kiss to such awkwardness in the space of an hour, two at the most?

Halfway between the two, she discovered when she checked her watch, and that was the answer. Too much had happened too quickly.

If the kitten hadn't made such a dramatic appearance they would have been able to sit quietly over supper. Dante would have explained about the flat, helped her find a room for the night and then tomorrow she'd have come by to thank him and maybe, hopefully, pick up on the fizz of attraction that had sizzled between them.

Instead, they'd veered between meltdown lust and awkwardness and in an effort to cover that she'd revealed way too much about herself.

Her mother, black hats—where on earth had all that come from? And that pheasant... She hadn't talked about that since her sisters had arrived home on the school bus to find her and Grandma singing a heartfelt *All Things Bright and Beautiful* over its resting place beneath a climbing rose.

'*Dio...*' Dante, the image of Angelica with her hands pressed against the window burning a hole in his brain, pulled open the bottom drawer of his desk and took out a bottle of grappa.

He poured himself a shot, tossed it back and for a moment he let the heat of it seep through his veins.

Close. He'd been within a whisper of touching her, had almost felt the down on her cheek rising to meet him as, lips softened, eyes closed, she'd anticipated a rerun of that kiss. He clenched his hand in an attempt to eradicate the memory.

He might have stepped back, walked out of the apartment before he did something unforgivable, but it hadn't stopped his imagination reacting to what had been a non-stop blast to his senses ever since she'd walked into his bar and stopped the conversation dead. The steely fresh air smell of her hair, snowflakes melting on her cheek, on crimson lips, she'd looked like something from a fairy tale. A lost princess stumbling out of the darkness.

He'd turned, their eyes had met and in that first look he'd forgotten the pain. The heartache...

And then she'd said, 'Via Pepone.'

He should have let Lisa deal with her because by then the complications were piling up, but that first look had fired a lightning charge through his senses, jump-starting them from hibernation as she walked towards him. As he'd touched her hand. As she'd removed her glove, removed her coat in a slow, tantalising reveal of the briefest little black dress.

His hand at her waist as he'd swept her out of the bar had sent a shock wave of heat surging through him and he hadn't been able to let it go.

He'd wanted to know how her cheek would feel beneath his fingers, wanted to taste her. He wanted to undress her, hold her against his naked skin, bury himself in her until he felt warm again.

What she'd said, how she'd looked at him when she'd stood by the window had been an invitation to take it all. Not a lost princess stumbling out of the night but something darker—an enchantress, a sorceress and if this had been a fairy tale he would already be doomed.

He shook his head.

Angelica Amery was simply a woman in need and that was the problem.

The spontaneity of that fall-into-bed moment had been real enough but Lisa's terrible—or possibly perfect—timing had wrecked that. They'd both had time to think about it and they'd lost the moment when a simple, unplanned elemental explosion of lust might have led anywhere or nowhere.

Worse, because she didn't know him, Angelica might well have thought he expected to share the bed he'd offered her.

Anything now would be tainted by that uncertainty and while his body, jolted out of stasis, might be giving him hell for walking away, he had to face himself in the shaving mirror in the morning.

Work. That had been the answer when Valentina had demanded that he forget Isola, that he walk away from what he couldn't change because, sooner or later, the old houses would come down and his father, or someone like him, would replace them with high-rise flats and office blocks. Work had been the answer when he'd allowed himself to be seduced by her sensual inducement to change his mind when he'd known in his heart that it was already over.

He called up the paper he'd been working on, his plan for the future of Isola, but the words on the screen kept dissolving into images that had nothing to do with preservation orders or affordable housing.

Angelica's hands—tapping the map with a blood-red nail...slowly unfastening tiny buttons...a fingertip stroking the head of the kitten.

Angelica's mouth lifted to kiss him, the black lace choker emphasising the length of her white neck.

Angelica's face as she stood beside him at the window watching the snow blanketing the city—

as she turned to him and he knew that all he had to do was reach out, touch her cheek and, for tonight at least, the dark emptiness of the void would be banished.

CHAPTER SIX

'In the winter dip your ice cream in sparkly rose-pink sprinkles.'
—from *Rosie's Little Book of Ice Cream*

CAFÉ ROSA WAS buzzing with morning activity. Men in working clothes were standing at the bar, a pastry in one hand, an espresso at their elbow. She was in Italy, where it cost more to sit down.

With so much whirling around in her mind Geli hadn't anticipated much sleep, but a soak in that huge bathtub with a splash of Lisa's luxurious lavender-scented bubbles and she'd gone out like a light the minute her head hit the pillow.

She'd taken the kitten's box into the bedroom with her in case it woke, hungry, in the night but it had been the sound of a distant door closing that woke her.

For a moment she hadn't known where she was but then the kitten had mewed and it had all come flooding back to her. The delayed flight, the non-existent apartment, Rattino. Dante…

She shook her head. Her life was complicated enough right now, without what might have become an awkward one-night stand. She might have inherited her mother's 'seize the day' genes—that she was feeling regret, the loss of something special missed, instead of relief proved that—but she'd had more sense.

She wrapped herself in her dressing gown, crossed to the window, rubbed the mist away with the edge of her hand. The early-morning sun was slanting across the city, lighting up colourful buildings—deep rose-pink, pale green, yellow; spotlighting a Madonna painted on a wall; glittering off the glass towers of high-rise blocks and snow-covered roofs.

Below her the pristine white of the snow had already been mashed to dirty slush by trucks bringing produce to the market stalls that had been erected along the street opposite. Everywhere there was colour, people wrapped up in thick coats and bright scarves, out and about getting on with their lives, and her heart gave a little skip of anticipation.

There was nothing like a good market to put a spring in the step!

She opened the bedroom door and stuck her head out.

'Dante?'

No response. Maybe he'd woken her when he'd left the flat. Not sure whether she was relieved or disappointed, she headed for the kitchen where she found a note pinned to the fridge door with a magnet.

Kitty comfort station in the utility room. Coffee and breakfast downstairs whenever you're ready. Lisa.

There was a litter tray ready and waiting for Rattino in the utility room, as well as two little plastic dishes filled with fresh minced chicken and milk and Geli found herself blinking rather rapidly at such thoughtfulness, such kindness. She'd read that in Isola she'd find the truest, most generous spirit of old Milan.

Clearly it was a fact.

She introduced Rattino to the first and watched as he dived into the second and then set his box on its side so that he could eat, sleep and do what came naturally at his leisure. Then she closed the door so that he couldn't wander and put the kettle on.

She found tea bags and dropped one in a mug and topped it up with boiling water. She found milk in the fridge and carried her must-have morning mug through to the bathroom. Hair dry, make-up in place, she layered herself in clothes that would see her through the day. A fine polo neck sweater, a narrow, high-waisted ankle-length skirt, stout Victorian-style lace-up boots, all black, which she topped with a rich burgundy velvet cut-away jacket that exactly matched her lipstick. She chose a steampunk-inspired pendant she'd made from the skeleton of a broken watch and, after a spin in front of the mirror to check that she was fluff-free, she went downstairs.

'*Ciao*, Geli!' Lisa called out as she spotted her. '*Come sta?*'

The men standing at the bar turned as one and stared.

'*Ciao, Lisa! Molto bene, grazie.* And Rattino thanks you for the litter tray. What do I owe you?'

She waved the offer away. 'Tell him to thank Dan. He called and asked me to pick it up on my way to work. Now, what can I get you? A latte?

Cappuccino? Or will you go hardcore with an espresso?'

'*Vorrei un cappuccino, grazie,*' she replied, testing her phrasebook Italian.

'*Buona sceita!*'

She called out the order to someone behind her, piled pastries on a plate and came out from behind the bar and headed for a table in the centre of the room.

'How are you this morning, Geli?'

'Pretty good, all things considered. I thought I'd be tossing and turning all night, but I'd be lying if I said I remember a thing after I closed my eyes.' She couldn't say the same about Lisa who, up close, looked as if she'd had a sleepless one. 'Thanks so much for offering me your spare room. It was a lifesaver.'

'No point in paying for a hotel room when there's an empty one going begging,' she said, pushing the pastries towards her. '*La prima colazione,*' she said, taking one. 'Otherwise known as cornettos. The perfect breakfast food.'

'Thanks.' Geli took one and her mouth was filled with crisp pastry and cream. 'Oh, good grief,' she spluttered. 'That's sinful.'

Lisa grinned. 'Start the day the way you mean

to go on,' she said then called out something in Italian to the men at the bar. They grinned, put down the empty cups they'd been nursing and made a move to go.

'What did you say to them?' Geli asked.

'To close their mouths before they catch flies.' She shook her head. 'You are going to be so good for business. Your make-up, your clothes—everything is perfect. Do you always make this much effort?'

'It goes with the territory. When you're a designer, you have to be your own walking advertisement.'

'It works for me. I'm no Milan fashionista, but I'd give my eye teeth for a jacket like yours.'

'I'll design a Dark Angel original for you when you come back from Australia. A very small thank you for being such a friend in need.'

'You don't have to do that.'

'It will be a totally selfish gift,' she assured her. 'You'll wear it and with those elegant shoulders you'll look fabulous.' She lifted her hands in a *job done* gesture.

'You're telling me that I'm going to be a walking shop dummy,' she said, grinning broadly.

'Walking and talking.'

'Oh, right. Everyone will want to know—' She stopped as Dante pulled out a chair and joined them.

Geli had wondered, as she'd taken her wake-up shower, if she'd imagined the attraction, or if it had simply been heightened by the drama of her arrival. A combination of being in Isola, being lost, the weather. Could anyone really hit all her hot buttons with no more than a look?

Apparently they could, even if it was a slightly crumpled, unsmiling version this morning.

'*Buongiorno*, Angelica,' he said. 'Did you sleep well?'

'*Buongiorno*, Dante,' she replied, her voice remarkably steady. It was the rest of her that felt as if it was shaking like a leaf. 'I slept amazingly well, under the circumstances.'

Dante, on the other hand, looked as if he'd been working all night and the urge to reach out and smooth the creases from his face was almost overwhelming. Fortunately, before she could do anything that idiotic he turned to Lisa.

'What will everyone want to know?' he asked.

'How on earth you managed to convince Geli that she should work for you,' she replied without a blush.

'Oh? And what is the answer?'

'You'll know that when you've persuaded her,' she said, getting to her feet. 'Off you go.'

'Lisa,' Angelica protested. 'My Italian is on the basic side of basic.'

'*No problema.* I might have an Italian father but I could barely utter a word when I arrived. Tell her, Dante,' she urged, turning a smile on her cousin that was so sweet it would give you toothache. 'There'll be a queue of regulars lining up to help her with the language and anything else she needs to make her stay in Isola a memorable experience before she can say *ciao*. Isn't that so?'

Geli, who had two older sisters, recognised one of those exchanges which, on the surface were exquisitely polite, while underneath there were seething undercurrents of hidden meaning.

'But you're family,' Geli protested, not sure what was going on, but not wanting to be in the middle of it.

'Unfortunately,' Dante said, his face expressionless. 'You can't fire family. It wasn't just the language; it was weeks before she could get an order straight or produce a decent espresso without me standing over her—'

Lisa snorted derisively and when he looked up

she lifted an eyebrow a mocking fraction right back at him. 'I'm sure Geli is *much* smarter than me.'

He looked thoughtful. 'But nowhere near as devious, it would seem.'

'It runs in the family,' Lisa replied, moving aside as the waiter arrived with a tray containing her cappuccino, an espresso for Dante and two bowls of something pale and creamy. 'I'll walk you through the job when you come back from the *commissariato*, Geli. *Buon appetito.*'

'*Sì...grazie...*' she said, then, unsure what to say to Dante, she indicated the bowl in front of her. 'What is this?'

'*Zabaglione.* Whipped eggs, cream, sugar, a little Marsala. I usually leave out the wine before midday,' he added, 'but it's bitter outside.'

'So this is antifreeze?'

He laughed and the tension, awkwardness was defused. 'Let's hope so.'

She dipped in her spoon and let a mouthful, sweet and warming, dissolve on her tongue. 'Oh, yum. Pastries and pudding for breakfast. My mother would have so approved.' He looked up. 'When anything bad happened she'd make us cupcakes for breakfast. With pink frosting and gold stars.'

'Pink?' His brow kinked in amusement. 'Really?'

'Black frosting is just creepy.' She shrugged. 'Except at Halloween.'

Dante looked as if he was about to say something but the bleep of an incoming text distracted her and she searched in her bag for her phone. 'Oh, no… '

'Problema?'

'You could say that. I shipped my heavy stuff before I left. Who knew it would get here so quickly?' She showed him the phone. 'I think the driver is trying to the find the non-existent address I gave them.'

Dante read the text then replied to it before handing it back. 'I told him to bring it here.'

'Oh… This is so embarrassing.'

'Why?'

'This was supposed to be me standing on my own two feet. Being grown-up. Self-sufficient.'

'Would you like me to tell them to leave it on the pavement?' he asked.

'No!' She shook her head. 'No…I'm sorry, I didn't mean to sound ungrateful but this is my first excursion into the unknown, the first time I've ever done anything totally on my own and it's all going wrong.'

'It's hardly your fault,' he assured her. 'And it's just until Monday.'

Monday? 'Yes, absolutely. I'll have found a room by then.'

'That's Monday, when you can move into the apartment I've found for you. I'm afraid that, like the job, it is only temporary, but it will give you a little breathing space while you get your-self sorted out.'

'You see? Like that,' Geli said and then swal-lowed. 'I'm sorry. That sounded so ungrateful.'

'Yes, it did.'

She groaned. 'I bet you wish you'd listened to the weather forecast and closed an hour earlier last night.' He didn't answer and she said, 'You're supposed to say no.'

The creases bracketing his mouth deepened slightly in what might just have been the prom-ise of a smile. 'I'm thinking about it.'

She rolled her eyes. 'Okay, how much is this temporary apartment you've found to go with my temporary job?'

'Just the utilities. It's only for a month while

Lisa and Giovanni are at the wedding, but it will give you time to look around.'

'Lisa and Giovanni?' She frowned. 'But I thought—'

'She wants me to give you a job so I offered her a deal. You get the job if she takes Giovanni as her plus one to her sister's wedding. They will need someone responsible to keep the pipes from freezing, make the place look lived in and feed the goldfish,' he added matter-of-factly. As if it was nothing. 'You are responsible, aren't you?'

'No goldfish has ever gone hungry on my watch,' she said, 'but why didn't Lisa tell me herself?'

'Because she wants you to stay here.'

'So that she doesn't have to take Giovanni?'

'No. His flight is booked.'

She went back over the conversation then shook her head. 'I seem to be missing something.'

'Lis believes that if we share the same apartment we'll inevitably fall into the same bed.'

The *zabaglione* took a diversion down her nose and Dante calmly handed her a paper napkin from the tray.

'That is outrageous.'

'I agree. I told her I never sleep with the staff, but apparently temps don't count.'

Never...? 'I wouldn't try that on an employment tribunal.'

'No,' he agreed with the wryest of smiles. 'And I did point out that, since you had nowhere else to go, any move on my part would be open to the worst interpretation.'

And any move on hers might be seen as...

'So you suggested moving me out so that I'm available?' She should be outraged. She was pretty sure she was outraged... 'I don't believe we're having this conversation. No, scrub that. I don't believe you had this conversation with Lisa.'

But it went a long way to explaining that edgy undercurrent between them this morning.

'*Mi dispiace*, Angelica. It is, as you say, quite outrageous.'

'So you applied a little pressure of your own?' And when, exactly, had he come up with that idea? 'How does Giovanni feel about that?'

'The man is in love. He'll do whatever she asks.' The thought did not appear to give him great pleasure.

'I imagine you're banking on the fact that after

a day of joy and celebration her family will realise that he doesn't have horns and a tail.'

'You're not convinced?'

'I don't know your family,' she said, 'and I don't know Giovanni, but I do know that weddings tend to be emotional affairs. There's the risk that, after a few glasses of the bubbly stuff, tongues will be loosened and fists will fly.'

'Maybe. Then they'll all get drunk, fling their arms around one another, vow eternal friendship and cry.'

'Or they'll all land in jail.'

'Or that.' He sat back. 'You don't have to take the job but if you'll just play along until they leave I'd be grateful.'

'I get that. What I don't understand is why throwing us together is so important to her.'

'We're doing each other a favour, Angelica. Does it matter if Lisa has her own agenda?'

Did it?

Lisa wanted to get them into bed together. Okay, so she'd been way ahead of her on her own account, but that was different. This was different... 'If you'll excuse me,' she said, sliding off her chair and standing up. It was time to leave. 'I'll pay for my breakfast and then I'll go and pack—'

He was on his feet, had caught her hand before she could move. 'Angelica...' She didn't pull her hand away, but she didn't look up at him. 'I haven't dated since my fiancée broke off our engagement a little over a year ago. Lisa thinks it's time I got back on the horse.'

He'd been dumped by the woman he loved? How unlikely was that? Then her brain got past the fact that any woman would dump him and she heard what he'd actually said.

'And I'm the horse?' she asked very quietly, aware that they were now the object of a dozen pairs of eyes. 'Gee, *grazie*, Dante. Or do I mean gee-gee *grazie*?' And, as everything suddenly fell into place, she took a step back. 'Is that what this has been about?' she demanded.

He tightened his grip on her hand. 'This?'

He'd known within minutes of her arrival that she was in trouble. All she'd seen was a man who could melt her underwear at twenty paces. All he'd seen was an opportunity. 'You've been using me from the beginning. Damn it, I should have known. If it looks too good...' she muttered, hurt, angry and feeling stupid. Again. 'Tell me, Dante, what would you have done without the kitten?'

'More to the point, what would you have done?' He closed the gap between them. 'You would still have needed somewhere to stay.' He reached up, touched her cheek with the tips of his fingers and the heat trickled through her, sweet and seductive as warm honey. 'There were two of us in that bedroom last night, Angelica. Which of us walked away?'

She flushed with embarrassment, well aware that it hadn't been her. That she'd wanted him with all the 'hang the consequences' recklessness of her Amery genes.

'I suppose I should be grateful that you weren't prepared to go that far,' she said, fighting the urge to lean into his hand. 'Oh, no, I forgot. You couldn't make a move in your own apartment. You need me off the premises so that it's not some totally sordid exchange that's open to misinter—'

'Basta!' His fingers slid through her hair, captured her head, shocking her into silence.

Around them, the café went quiet. He looked up and instantly everyone found they had somewhere else they needed to be. Then he turned back to her.

'I'm sorry, Angelica. You're absolutely right. We are both using you for our own ends but here's the deal. You get an apartment rent-free for a month and a temporary job if you want it. And, no matter what my cousin hopes might happen, there are no strings attached to either offer.'

'No strings? Well, golly, that's all right then.'

'Lis thinks she's helping,' he said, 'but I'm not ready for any kind of relationship. I don't know if I ever will be.'

'I don't imagine she's envisaging a "relationship",' she replied, making ironic quote marks with her fingers. 'Just a quick gallop to shake out the cobwebs. I'm a temp, remember?'

'Dio...' he said a touch raggedly. At her nape, his hand softened but he didn't remove it and, despite her anger, she didn't step away. 'I was trying to be honest with you, Angelica. Nothing hidden. No con—'

Behind her, the café door opened, letting in a blast of cold air. 'Signora Amery?'

'Would you rather I'd prettied it up?' he insisted. 'Lied to you?'

Behind Dante, she saw Lisa watching them anxiously.

Above her, Dante's face was unreadable.

She had left Longbourne determined to shake up her life, grab every experience that came her way. So far, Isola was delivering on all fronts. Make that all fronts but one. Not a problem. She was here to work, to learn, to grow as a designer, an artist. A little hot sex would have been a bonus but she wasn't looking for anything as complicated, as involving as a relationship. She had that in common with her mother, too. And, apparently, Dante.

The man at the door called out something in Italian and Lisa said, 'Geli...someone wants you.'

'Oh, for heaven's sake,' she muttered, then turned to the man standing in the doorway, '*Sono Angelica Amery.*'

'I'll see your boxes safely stored while you get your coat,' Dante said as the driver went to unload them. 'We'll go to the police station as soon as it's done.' He needed a little breathing space to recover from the sensory overload of being in close proximity to Angelica. A little cold air in his lungs.

'Would you like me to bring your jacket?' she asked.

'*Grazie*, Angelica. Thank you.' For a moment neither of them moved and the long look that passed between them acknowledged that it wasn't just the jacket he was thanking her for.

The last of the boxes was being stacked in the room opposite his office when she returned, dressed for the weather in the head-turning coat with pockets big enough to conceal a small animal. She'd added a scarf which she'd coiled in some fashionable loop around her neck and a black velvet beret with a glittering spider hat pin to fasten it in place.

Lisa was right. She certainly knew how to make an entrance. She was going to be a sensation at the *commissariato*.

'What is all this stuff?' he asked, indicating the boxes as she handed him his jacket and scarf.

'My Mac. A couple of collapsible worktables,' she said, walking around the boxes, touching each one in turn as she identified the contents. 'My drawing board, easel, paints, brushes, sketch pads.' The long full skirt of her coat brushed against the cartons as she moved among them.

'You intend to paint as well as design clothes?' he asked.

'Maybe...I haven't done anything serious since I switched to fashion for my post-grad. And I've been busy with the ice cream parlour franchise.' She stopped and bent to check a label. 'My sewing machines are in this one. And my steamer.' She looked up. 'I'll need to unpack the fragile stuff to make sure it's all survived the journey.'

'No problem. What about these?' he asked, indicating some of the larger boxes.

'Material, trimmings, buttons. It looks a lot when you see it in a small space,' she said.

'Buttons? You brought buttons with you? You can buy them in Italy,' he pointed out.

She smiled at that. 'I know, and I can't wait to go shopping, but these are buttons I've collected over the years. Some are very old. Some, like these—' she touched one of the tiny jet buttons at her waist and he tried not to think about the way she'd unfastened them last night...one by one '—are quite valuable.'

'Right.' He struggled with a dry mouth. 'Well, the bad news is that you're never going to get all this into Lisa's tiny one-bed flat.'

'Is there any good news?'

'This room isn't being used. You can work here until you find workshop space. Or a flat large enough to accommodate all this.'

'But—'

'I'll move these out of your way.' He indicated the few dusty boxes he'd pushed to one side. 'Will it do?'

'It's perfect, Dante, but we have to discuss rent.'

He'd anticipated that. 'No discussion necessary. In return for a month's lease, you can design an ice cream parlour for me. Whether you consider that good news is for you to decide. Shall we go?'

CHAPTER SEVEN

'There are no recipes for leftover ice cream.'
—from *Rosie's Little Book of Ice Cream*

THE POLICE STATION was noisy, crowded, and Italian policewomen, Geli discovered to her delight, really did wear high heels.

'How on earth do they run in them?' she asked. Anything to break the silence as she waited with Dante for a detective to come and talk to them.

'Run?'

'Never mind,' she said. 'Stupid question. They're all so glamorous I imagine the crooks put up their hands and surrender for the sheer pleasure of being handcuffed and patted down by them.'

She swallowed, unable to believe she'd actually said anything so sexist.

Dante said nothing. He'd said very little other than, 'Take care…' as they'd walked along the snow-packed street.

'Dante!' A detective approached them, shook him by the hand. *'Signora...?'*

'Giorgio, may I introduce Signora Angelica Amery?' Dante said, then, 'Angelica—Commissario Giorgio Rizzoli. Giorgio...' Dante explained the situation in Italian too rapid for her to catch more than a word or two. *'Inglese...* Via Pepone...'

'Signora Amery...' The Commissario placed his hand against his heart. *'Mi dispiace...'*

'He's desolate that you have had such a terrible experience,' Dante translated. 'We are to go through to his office, where he'll take the details, although he's sure you will understand that the chances of recovering your money are very small.'

'Tell him that I understand completely and that I'm very sorry to take up his valuable time.'

Reporting the crime took a very long time. Apart from the fact that everything had to be translated, it seemed that every officer on duty, from a cadet who was barely old enough to shave to one who was well past retiring age, had some pressing matter that only the Commissario could resolve. He was extraordinarily patient, introducing each of his men to her, explaining what had happened and smiling benevolently as each one welcomed her to Isola, offered whatever assistance was in their power to give and held her hand sympathetically while gazing into her eyes.

Dante, in the meantime, gazed out of the window as she repeated the well-rehearsed phrase, *'Mi dispiace, parli lentamente per favore...'*— begging them to speak slowly. If she didn't know better, she would have thought he was afraid to catch her eye in case he laughed. It gave her a warm feeling. As if they were partners in a private joke.

'Well, you promised me it would be an experience and I have to admit that it was almost worth being robbed,' she said as they paused on the steps, catching their breath as they hit the cold air. 'Tell me, are the women officers notably more efficient than the men?' He took her arm as they made their way down the steps, despite the fact that they had been cleared and gritted. 'Only I noticed none of them needed assistance.'

'I think you know the answer to that.'

He wasn't smiling and released her arm the moment they hit the slushy, slippery pavement, keeping a clear distance between them as they walked back to the café, his face, his body so stiff that he looked as if he'd crack in two.

After about twenty paces she couldn't stand it another moment and stopped. 'Dante, last night...' He'd gone a couple of steps before he realised she wasn't with him and glanced back. 'This morning...' She swallowed. 'I just wanted you to know that I'm truly grateful for everything. I won't do or say anything to mess up Lisa's plans.'

He turned to face her. 'I appreciate that,' he said stiffly.

'And I'll design you the prettiest ice cream parlour imaginable. If you're serious about the workshop space?'

'It's yours, but this isn't the weather to be standing around in the street discussing interior decoration.'

She didn't move.

He shrugged. 'There's a small room at the back of Café Rosa that opens onto the garden. When I saw your designs it occurred to me that an American ice cream parlour might go down well with the younger element.'

'In that case, forget pretty—it had better be nineteen-fifties cool.'

'Maybe. Will your sister object to me borrowing her ideas?'

'There's no copyright in ideas,' she said. 'She borrowed the concept from the US after all and you won't be calling it Knickerbocker Gloria, using her branding or copying her ices. You'll be using gelato rather than ice cream, I imagine?'

'You're getting technical.'

'Just thinking ahead. Will you make your own *gelato* or buy it in, for instance? Is there anyone local who would make specials for you?'

'Good question. I'll think about it. Shall we go?'

'Yes...' She took a step, stopped again. 'No.' There was something she had to say. 'I want you to know that I understand why you were being completely—if rather brutally—honest with me this morning.'

'Do you?'

'You said it's no con—at least where I'm concerned. Lisa, well, that's between you and her.'

'Is that it?'

'Yes...' She rolled her eyes; he really wasn't helping... 'No.' He said nothing, although his eyebrows spoke volumes. But he waited. 'You might want to relax a little, walk a little closer, try and find a smile from somewhere because right now we look as if we're in the middle of a fight rather than about to fall into bed.'

'Do we?' And for a moment the question, loaded with unspoken reference to how close they'd come to the latter, hung there. Then he stuck his hands in his pockets, looked somewhere above her head. 'I owe you an apology, too.'

'If it's about the horse thing,' she said quickly as they continued walking, 'the least said the better.'

'Lisa put the words in my head last night and they leapt out when I wasn't paying attention,' he said and stuck out his elbow, inviting her to slide her arm beneath it. Her turn to do the thing with the eyebrows and he raised a wintry smile. 'You said it, Angelica—we're in this together.'

'Right.' She tucked her arm in his and he drew her closer, no doubt glad of warmth. 'And forget about the horse. I shouldn't be so touchy. I don't know what I'd have done last night if you hadn't been so kind.'

'You'd have managed,' he said as they walked back towards Café Rosa. 'You're a resourceful woman.'

'I'm glad you think so because I'd rather like

to put my resourcefulness to the test,' she said as they reached the piazza. 'Will the bartending lesson keep for an hour?'

'Take all the time you need. Lisa managed to drag hers out for weeks.'

'How?' she asked. The fancy barista stuff might take time to master but the basics weren't exactly rocket science.

'I was too wrapped up in my own misery at the time to realise that she was playing the idiot in order to keep me busy. Doing her best to take my mind off Valentina.'

'Valentina? Your fiancée?'

'She's not my anything.' In the low slanting sun his face was all dark shadows. 'She's married to someone else.'

'So soon?' Not the most tactful response but the words had been shocked out of her.

'My father was ready to give her everything I would not.' Grey... His face was grey... 'And it seems that she was pregnant.'

His father?

They'd reached the first market stall and, while she was still trying to get her head around what he'd told her, he unhooked his arm and stepped away. 'Give me your phone and I'll put my number in your contacts.'

Geli handed over her phone but her brain was still processing his shocking revelation.

Valentina had been cheating on him with his father? No wonder he'd withdrawn into himself or that Lisa was so worried about him.

Dante slipped off a glove, programmed in his number and handed her back her phone. 'Give me a call if you need any help haggling over the price of designer clothes and shoes.'

'What...?'

He'd dropped an emotional bombshell and was now casually discussing the price of shoes. But there had been nothing casual or throwaway about his earlier remark. His mention of Valentina had been deliberate; he'd chosen to tell her what had happened before someone else—before Lisa—filled her in on the gossip. And then, just as deliberately because he didn't want to talk about it, he'd changed the subject.

'Oh, yes. *Grazie*,' she said, doing her best to sound equally casual as she dropped the phone back in her pocket. 'I love looking around a new market but I'm afraid that clothes and shoes are on hold until I find out if the bank is going to

refund my money.' Concentrate on the most im-
mediate problem. 'My first priority is to take a
walk back to where I found Rattino and see if
anyone is missing him. Do people put up "lost
pet" notices around here?'

'I can't say I've noticed any. I suppose we could
put up some "found" ones?'

'That's probably a lot wiser than knocking on
strangers' doors when I barely speak a word of
Italian,' she agreed.

'Not just wiser,' he said, 'it would be a whole
lot safer. Do not, under any circumstances, do
that on your own.'

'You could come with me.'

'Let's stick with the posters. Can I leave you
to take a look around the market without getting
into any trouble while I take a photograph of the
rat and run off a few posters? I'll come and find
you when they're done.'

'Trouble?' she repeated, looking around at the
bustling market. 'What trouble?'

'If you see anything with four legs, looking
lost, walk away.'

Geli explored the market, using her phone to take
pictures of the colourful stalls and sending them

to her sisters. Proof that she'd arrived, was safe and doing what came naturally.

She tried out her Italian, exchanging greetings, asking prices, struggling with the answers until her ear began to tune in to the language of the street as opposed to the carefully enunciated Italian on her teach yourself Italian course.

Despite her intention to simply browse, she was unable to resist some second-hand clothes made from the most gorgeous material and was browsing a luscious selection of ribbon and beads on a stall selling trimmings when Dante found her.

The stallholder, a small, plump middle-aged woman so bundled up that only her face was showing, screamed with delight and flung her arms around him, kissing his cheeks and rattling off something in rapid Italian. Dante laughed and then turned to introduce her.

'Livia, *questa è la mia amica*, Angelica. Angelica, this is Livia.'

Geli offered her hand. '*Piacere*, Livia.'

Her tentative Italian provoked a wide smile and another stream of unintelligible Italian as Livia closed both of her hands around the box of black beads she'd been looking at and indicated that she should put it in her bag.

'I sorted out her traders' licence a few months ago,' Dante explained. 'It's her way of saying thank you.'

'She should be thanking you.'

'I don't have a lot of use for beads and, since you are my friend, it would make her happy if you took them. You can buy something from her another day.'

'*Grazie mille*, Livia,' she said. 'Will you tell her I love her stall, Dante, and that I'll come back and buy from her very soon.'

He said something that earned her a huge smile then, after more hugs and kisses for both of them, Dante took the carrier she was holding and peered into it.

'You changed you mind about window-shopping, I see?'

She shrugged. 'I've got a job, rent-free accommodation for a month and a workshop that I'm paying for with my time. And now I've got some fabulous material to work with, just as soon as I unpack my sewing machine.'

'Do you need more time?' He looked around. 'I believe there are still a few black things left—' She jabbed her elbow in his ribs and he grinned. 'I guess not.' He took a sheaf of papers from the roomy pocket of his waxed jacket. 'Shall we get this done?'

She took one and looked at the photograph Dante had taken of the kitten. 'He's quite presentable now that he's clean and dry. *Trovato*... Found?' He nodded. '*Contattare* Café Rosa. And the telephone number. Well, that's direct and to the point. Uh-oh...' She looked up as something wet landed on the paper and the colours of the ink began to run into one another as more snow began to fall. 'If we put them out now they'll be a soggy mess in no time,' Geli said. 'Have you got a laminator?'

'No.'

'Fortunately, I packed mine.'

While Dante, wrapped up against the weather, left on his mission to stick up the laminated posters of the lost kitten, Geli called her bank's fraud office and passed on the crime number the Commissario had given her.

'Okay?' Lisa asked, handing her a long black apron.

She shrugged. 'I've done everything I can.' She tied the apron over her clothes and watched Lisa's demonstration of the Gaggia and then produced, one after the other, a perfect espresso, latte and cappuccino.

Lisa, arms folded, watched her through narrowed eyes. 'You've done this before.'

'I was a student for four years. My sisters paid me for the work I did for them, but paints, material and professional sewing machines do not come cheap. Then, as now, I needed a job.'

'Right, Little Miss Clever Clogs, you've got your first customer.' She indicated a man standing at the counter. 'Go get him.'

Geli took a deep breath. *'Ciao, signor. Che cosa desidera?'* she asked.

He smiled. *'Ciao, signora...* Geli,*'* he added, leaning closer to read the name tag that Lisa had pinned to her apron. *'Il sono* Marco.*'*

'Ciao, Marco. *Piacere. Che cosa desidera?'* she repeated.

'Vorrei un espresso, per favore,' he said. Then, having thanked her for it, *'Che programme ha per stasera? Le va di andare a bere qualcosa?'*

The words might not have been familiar, but the look, the tone certainly were and she turned to Lisa. 'I think I'm being hit on. How do I say I'm washing my hair?'

'He wants to know if you have any plans for

tonight and, if not, can he buy you a drink. So good for business…' she murmured.

'Definitely washing my hair.'

Lisa gave him the bad news and he smiled ruefully, shrugged and drank his coffee.

'What did you say?'

'That you're working tonight. Why?' she asked, thoughtfully. 'Have you changed your mind? He is rather cute.'

'Very cute.'

'Well, he knows where you'll be tonight. Maybe he'll come back.'

'Does that mean I've passed the interview?'

'When can you start?'

'It had better be this evening, don't you think? I wouldn't want Marco to think I was lying.'

'Heaven forbid. Come on, I'll run you through the routine and then you'd better go and put your feet up. It tends to get busy on a Saturday night.'

Half an hour later, Geli said, 'Can I make a hot chocolate to go? I'll pay for it.'

'There's no need. Staff get fed and watered.'

'It's not for me. One of the stallholders I met this morning is a friend of Dante's—'

'They're all his friends when they want something,' she said, pulling a face.

'Are they? Oh, well, anyway, she gave me some beads so I thought I'd take her a hot drink.'

'That's thoughtful, but it's on the house,' she said as Geli made the chocolate and poured it into a carry out cup with a lid. 'You don't know how grateful I am that you're staying, Geli. I really didn't want to leave Dante on his own.'

'Hardly on his own. He seems to know everyone.'

'Everyone knows him. They come to him for help because he'll stand up for them, fight their corner against bureaucracy and lead their campaigns to save this place from the developers. They don't care what it costs him. You're different.'

Geli shrugged, not wanting to get into exactly how different it was. The situation was already awkward enough.

'I mean it,' Lisa said. 'You're the first woman he's shown the slightest interest in for over a year and it hasn't been for lack of attention from women wanting to comfort him. He was engaged—'

'He told me what happened,' she said, cutting Lisa off mid gossip.

'You see? He never talks about that. I don't suppose he told you that they were both punishing him for not doing what they wanted?'

'Punishing him?' Geli shook her head. 'I…I imagined an affair.'

'Nothing so warm-blooded.' Lisa rubbed a cloth over the chrome. 'It hit him very hard.'

So hard that he couldn't envisage another relationship. That was why he'd told her. Not to forestall gossip, but so that she'd understand his reluctance to follow through on the obvious attraction. The classic 'It's not you, it's me…' defence.

'I'm just saying…' Lisa concentrated on polishing an invisible smudge. 'I wouldn't want you to be hurt.'

Really? A bit late to be worrying about that, Lisa…

Geli shook her head. 'I'm not interested in commitment. My sisters have all that happy-ever-after stuff, baby thing well covered. I'm my mother's child.'

She frowned. 'Your mother?'

'She didn't believe in long-term relationships. My sisters and I all have different fathers. At least we assume we do, since we all look quite different.'

'You don't know your father?'

'She used sperm donors.' It was her standard response to anyone interested enough to ask. Spilling out the truth to Dante had been a rare exposure. But then everything about Dante was rare. 'So much less bother, don't you think?'

'Um…' She'd rendered Lisa speechless? That had to be a first… 'Okay. Well, I suggest you come down at seven, while it's still quiet, and you can shadow Matteo. He'll look after you until you get the hang of things. Hold on…' She reached behind her. 'Take the menu to familiarise yourself with it.' She wrote something on the bottom. 'And that should deal with anyone pestering you for a date, although a shrug and *non capisco* will get you out of most situations.'

'Like this?' She shrugged and, putting on a breathy Italian accent, said, *'Non capisco.'*

Lisa grinned. 'Say it like that and I refuse to be responsible!'

Saturday night at Café Rosa was non-stop service of food and drink to the accompaniment of the jazz quartet from the night before. Everyone was very patient with her and Matteo caught any potential disasters before they happened. She had a couple more offers of a drink and dinner, which she managed to dodge without incident, although once Lisa was away there was no need to pretend that she and Dante might become an item—

'Geli...' She turned to find Lisa holding a tray loaded with coffee, water and a *panino*.

'You can take your break now. Will you give this to Dan on your way upstairs? And remind him that it's Saturday night. All work and no play...' She looked around. 'We seem to be between rushes at the moment. Take your time.'

Dante heard Angelica coming—it was disconcerting how quickly he'd come to recognise her quick, light step—but he didn't look up as she opened the door. If she saw he was busy she might not stop. His head might be telling him not to get involved, but his body wasn't listening and he needed to keep his distance.

'Lisa sent you some supper,' she said, placing it on the table behind his desk.

Of course she had. Any excuse that would throw them together...

He grunted an acknowledgement and continued to pound away at the keyboard.

'It's not good for you, you know.'

'What isn't?'

'Eating while you work.' Angelica backed up and propped herself on the edge of his desk. 'You'll get indigestion, heartburn and stomach ulcers.'

Nothing compared with what her bottom, inches from his hand, was doing to him. 'Haven't you got a café full of customers?'

'I'm on my break.' He continued typing, although it was unlikely he was making any sense. 'Lisa expects me to sit on your knee and ruffle your hair while I tell you about all the men who've hit on me this evening.'

'Did she say that?'

'Not in so many words, but she told me to remind you that all work and no play makes Dante very dull. And she told me to take my time. Of course, it could be that I'm so useless she's desperate to get me out of the way for half an hour.'

'Are you useless?'

'Not totally.'

No. He'd heard all about her virtuoso performance on the Gaggia from a very smug Lisa.

He stopped pretending to work and looked up. She'd swathed herself in one of the Café Rosa's long black aprons and her hair was tied back with a velvet ribbon. She looked cool and efficient but that full crimson mouth would turn heads at fifty paces.

'How many men?' he asked.

'Let's see. There was Roberto.' She held up her hand, fingers spread wide and ticked him off on a finger. 'Dark hair, blue eyes, leather biker jacket. *"Andiamo in un posto più tranquillo..."*' she said in a low, sexy voice.

'I'd advise against going anywhere with him, noisy or quiet.'

'He's bad?'

'His wife is away, looking after her sick mother.'

'What a jerk,' she said, using a very Italian gesture to dismiss him. 'What about Leo? He wanted to "friend" me on Facebook. Was that a euphemism for something else, do you think?'

'That you're thinking it suggests you already know.'

'Men! All they want is sex. Doesn't anyone ask a girl out on a proper date any more?'

'A proper date?' he asked.

'The kind where a man picks a girl up from her home, takes her to the movies, buys her popcorn and they hold hands in the dark—'

'Was that it?' He cut her off, trying not to think

about Angelica in the dark with some man who might be holding her hand in the cinema but would have his mind on where else he was going to hold her when he got her home.

'What? Oh, no. Gennaro was very sweet, but I'm not looking for a father figure, and Nic, the guy who plays the saxophone, said *"Ti amo..."* in the most affecting way, but I think that was because I'd just taken him a beer.'

'That'll do it every time for Nic; even so, that's quite a fan club you've got there. Are any of them going to get lucky?'

'With Lisa keeping a close eye on me? She's doing a great job of protecting your interests.'

'She doesn't trust my personal charm to hold you in thrall?'

'I'm down there and you're up here working.' She lifted her shoulders, sketching a shrug. 'Out of sight, out of mind.' She blew away a wisp of hair that had escaped its tie. 'Did I mention Marco? He came in this afternoon when Lisa was showing me the ropes. I made him an espresso. He's downstairs now...' She stopped. 'You don't want to hear this when you're so obviously busy. I hadn't realised running a bar involved so much bureaucracy.'

'There's enough to keep me fully occupied, but I'm working on a development plan for Isola. One that doesn't involve pulling down historic streets,' he added.

'Oh, I see. Well, that's seriously important work and I'm disturbing you.'

Without a doubt...

'Don't forget your supper,' she said, rubbing the tip of her thumb across her lower lip. 'Is my lipstick convincingly smudged, do you think?' As she leaned forward so that he could give her his opinion, the top of her apron gaped to offer a glimpse of black lace beneath the scoop top of the black T-shirt she was wearing. It was clinging to soft white breasts and if that was the view that customers were getting as she served them it was hardly any wonder that she was getting hit on. 'Maybe I should muss up my hair a bit?'

'You want Lisa to think that we've been making out over my desk?'

'I'm doing my best to convince her that we're struggling to keep our hands off each other. Without a lot of help, I might add—'

As she reached up to tease out a strand, he caught her wrist.

'You want your hair mussed?' he asked, his voice sounding strange, as if he'd never heard it before.

She said nothing, but the tip of her tongue appeared briefly against softly parted lips, her pupils widened, black as her hair, swallowing up the silver-grey of her eyes and the catch in her breath was answered by his body's clamour to touch her, take her.

For a moment neither of them moved then he released her wrist, reached for the ribbon holding her hair and, as he tugged it loose, the silken mass fell forward, brushing against his face, enveloping him in the intimacy of its scent as she slid into his lap.

His fingers slipped through it as he cradled her head, angling his mouth to tease her lips open and, as he brushed against the sensitive nerve endings at her nape, a tiny moan—more vibration than sound—escaped her lips, her body softened against him and his tongue was swathed in hot sweet satin.

With one hand tangled in her hair, the other sought out the gap between her T-shirt and the black ankle-length skirt that hid her fabulous legs, sliding over satin skin to cradle her lace-covered breast, touch her candy-hard nipple.

She wanted this, he wanted it and he was a fool not to taste her, touch her, bury himself deep inside her—over his desk, on the floor, in his bed. It had nothing to do with emotion, feelings; this was raw, physical need.

It was just sex—

The four words slammed through his body like an ice storm. Colder than the snow-covered Dolomites.

'It was just sex...'

The last words Valentina had said to him.

'Okay, that should do it,' he said, lifting her from his lap and setting her on her feet before swinging his chair back to face his laptop. 'If that's all, I want this on the Minister's desk first thing on Monday.'

She didn't move but he didn't have to look to know that her hair was loose about her shoulders, her swollen lips open in a shocked O, her expression that of a kicked puppy. The image was imprinted indelibly on his brain.

He didn't expect or wait for an answer but began pounding on the keyboard as if nothing had happened while she backed out of the room, then turned and ran up the stairs. Kept pounding until he heard the door bang shut on the floor above and his fingers froze above the keyboard.

He stared at the screen, the cursor blinking an invitation to delete the rubbish he'd just written. Instead, he slumped back in the chair, dragging his hands over his face, rubbing hard to eradicate every trace of Angelica Amery. It didn't work. The scent of her skin, her hair was on his hands, in his lungs and, as he wiped the back of his hand over his mouth in an attempt to eradicate the honeyed taste of her lips, it came away bearing traces of crimson lipstick.

It would be two more days before Angelica moved out.

They were going to be two very long days and right now he needed air—fresh, clean, cold air—to blow her out of his head.

CHAPTER EIGHT

'You can't buy happiness but you can buy ice cream...which is much the same thing.'
—from *Rosie's Little Book of Ice Cream*

GELI'S RACING PULSE, pounding heartbeat said, *Run—run for your life*. Falling in lust with a man who had made it clear not once, not twice but three times that while he might be aroused—and he had certainly been aroused—he was not interested in any kind of relationship was a recipe for disaster.

Sharing an apartment with that man, working with him was never going to work.

She threw open her bedroom window, stuck her head out and filled her lungs with icy air, hoping that it would cool not just her skin but freeze the heat from the inside out.

What was it about Dante Vettori that made her lose her wits? What had started out as a little teasing had ended with his arms around her, his mouth on hers, his hands spread wide over her skin. She shivered and pressed her hand hard against her breast, where his touch had created a shock of pleasure that racketed around her body like a pinball machine, lighting up every sensory receptor she had.

Maybe she should suggest some straightforward recreational sex so they could both get it out of their systems. No strings. Except if he'd been a 'no strings' kind of guy he'd have been out there, taking anything on offer in an attempt to obliterate the heartbreak. A man who looked like Dante would not have been short of offers.

If he'd been a 'no strings' kind of guy they would have been naked right now.

He needed something more than that. Or maybe something less. Someone who didn't want anything from him but was just there…

She was good at that. She'd been rescuing broken creatures ever since she'd picked up that injured pheasant. She'd never tried rescuing a broken person before but there was no difference. They were edgy, scared and you had to earn their trust, too. No sudden moves. No demands…

She checked on Rattino, sat on the floor rubbing his tiny domed head, while she sipped iced water, rolled the glass against her mouth to cool her swollen lips and heated libido.

Having stretched the taking her time instruction to the limit, she found a clip and fastened back her hair, straightened her clothes, applied a fresh coat of lipstick. It was time to get back to work…

Dante was standing in the middle of the sitting room. He was wearing his jacket, had a bright red scarf around his neck and in his hands he was holding a battered cardboard box.

For a moment they stared at one another, then he said, 'I found this on the back doorstep.'

'On the doorstep?' What was he doing on the doorstep when he was so busy writing a report…?

'I needed some fresh air,' he said.

You and me both, mister, she thought, taking a step closer so that she could see what was in the box.

'Oh, kittens.' Two of them, all eyes, huddled together in the corner. 'Your notice appears to have worked.'

'I was under the impression that its purpose was to find the owner of Rattino so that we could return him to the bosom of his family,' he said, unimpressed. 'Not have the rest of his family dumped on our doorstep.'

She looked up. *Our doorstep...*

'In an ideal world,' she said, returning to the kittens, picking each one up in turn and checking it over for any sign of injury before replacing it in the box. 'They're thin but otherwise seem in good shape.'

'I imagine their mother is a stray who didn't come back from a hunting trip.'

'It seems likely. And would explain why Rattino went looking for food. He is the biggest. So what do you think?'

'What do I think?'

'Shall we call the black one Mole and the one with stripes Badger? We already have Ratty?' she prompted. '*Wind in the Willows*? It's a classic English children's book,' she explained when he made no response. 'Or would you prefer Italian names?'

'I think...' He took a breath. 'I think I'll go and take down those notices before anyone else decides to leave a box of unwanted kittens on the doorstep.'

'Right. Good plan. I'll, um, feed these two,' she said as he headed for the door. 'Introduce them to the amenities. Will you keep an eye out for their mother, while you're out? She wouldn't have abandoned them.'

'If she's been hit by a car—'

'You're right. She may be lying hurt somewhere,' she said. 'Hang on while I see to these two and I'll come with you. I know the kind of places she'll crawl into.'

Geli had no doubt that Dante would rather be on his own but, rather than waste his breath, he said, 'I'll go and tell Lisa that she's going to have to manage without you.'

'You'll make her evening.'

'No doubt.' His tone left her under no illusion that she wasn't making his. 'Wrap up well. It's freezing out there.'

Twenty minutes later, having fed the kittens, reunited them with their brother and changed her flat working shoes for a pair of sturdy boots, she was walking with Dante along the street where she'd found Rattino.

'Urban cats have a fairly limited range,' she explained, stopping every few yards to check doorways and explore the narrow street that had given her a fright the night she'd arrived. 'They avoid fights by staying out of each other's way whenever possible. Will you hold this?'

'Where is your glove?' he demanded when she handed him her flashlight and began to turn over boxes with her bare hand.

'In my pocket. I held the kittens so she'd smell them on me but she's not here—'

She broke off as he took her icy hand and tucked it into his own roomy fleece-lined glove so that their hands were palm to palm. 'Now we'll both smell of her kittens.'

She looked up at him. 'Good thinking.'

'I'm glad you approve,' he said and the shadows from the street lights emphasised the creases as, unexpectedly, he smiled.

Oh, boy... She turned away to grab one of the notices from a nearby lamp post and saw the wooden barriers surrounding the construction site where Via Pepone used to be.

'There,' she said. 'If she's survived, she'll be in there.'

'Are you certain?'

'As certain as I can be. Disturbed ground, displaced rodents, workmen dropping food scraps, lots of places to hide. Perfect for a mother with three hungry kittens. Maybe someone working on the site knew they were there and when he saw the notice brought them to us.'

'That makes sense.' He walked across to the site entrance and tried the gate. It did not budge.

'Is there a night watchman?' she asked.

'It's the twenty-first century.' He looked up at the cameras mounted on high posts. 'It's all high-tech security systems and CCTV monitored from a warm office these days.'

'Okaaay.' She reluctantly removed her hand from his glove and fished in her pocket for her own. 'In that case you'll have to give me a bunk-up so that I can climb over.'

'Alarms?' he reminded her. 'CCTV.'

'Which will deal with the problem of how I'd climb back out again with an injured cat. And the local *polizia* are so helpful. I'm sure they'll drive me to the vet before they arrest me.'

'Drive you to the vet, send out for hot chocolate to keep you warm and raise a collection to pay the vet's bill, I have no doubt. But you've had your quota of excitement for this week.'

'Well, that's a mean thing to say.' Their breath mingled in the freezing air and she pulled on her glove before she did something really exciting, like grabbing his collar and pulling him down to warm their freezing lips. 'Okay, your turn. What do you suggest?'

'I suppose I could climb over the fence and get arrested.'

'Your life is that short of excitement?'

'Not since you and that wretched kitten arrived.'

'You can thank me later. Any other ideas?' She waited. 'I sensed an *or* in there somewhere.'

He shrugged, looked somewhere above her head. 'Or I could make a phone call and get the security people to let us in.'

'Maybe sooner rather than later,' she suggested, stamping her feet.

He looked down at her for a long moment, then took out his cellphone, thumbed a number on his fast dial list and walked away down the street as he spoke to whoever answered. The conversation was brief and he wasn't smiling as he rejoined her.

'Someone will be here in a few minutes.'

'Well, that's impressive.'

'You think so?'

He looked up at the floodlit boarding high above the fence with an artist's impression of the office block that would replace Via Pepone.

It bore the name of the construction company in huge letters. Beneath, smaller, was the name of the developer.

Vettori SpA.

Oh... 'That's not a coincidence, is it?' she said.

'My great-grandfather started the business after the war, repairing bomb-damaged buildings, working every hour God gave to save enough money to buy some land and build a small block of flats. My grandfather took over a thriving construction company and continued to expand the business until a heart attack forced him to retire and he handed it over to my father.'

This was his father's project? 'Was that who you called just now? Your father?'

Before he could answer, a security patrol van drew up in a spray of dirty snow. The driver leapt out, exchanged a few words with Dante in rapid Italian and then unlocked the small personal door set in the gates.

'Take care, Angel,' Dante said, taking her hand as they stepped through after him.

Angel? She turned and looked up at him.

'A construction site is a hazardous place,' he said.

'Yes...' With the ground frozen, no work had

been done in the last couple of days and, as the patrolman shone his flashlight slowly across the site, there were few footprints to mar the pristine snow. Then she saw something... 'There!' She snatched her hand away to point to where the light picked up a disturbance in the snow. Not paw prints but a wider trail marked by darker patches of blood where an animal had dragged herself across the ground, desperate to get back to her babies. 'She's hurt.'

'Wait...'

She ignored Dante, running across the yard, using her own small flashlight to follow the trail until she reached the place where the cat had wedged herself under pallets piled with building materials.

'Let me do this.' Dante knelt beside her, but she'd already stripped off her gloves and was holding out her hands so that the cat could smell her kittens. Crooning and chirruping, she dragged herself towards the scent until Geli could reach her and lift her gently from her hiding place. '*Dio*... She's a mess.'

'We need to keep her warm. Take my scarf,' she urged, but Dante pulled off his beautiful red cashmere scarf and wrapped it around the poor creature. 'We need to get her to a vet,' she said.

Dante looked at this angel, so passionate, so full of compassion.

He called the vet and then asked the security guard to drive them to his office. 'He'll meet us there. Come on; it'll be a squeeze, but it's not far,' he said, holding the door so that she could slide into the passenger seat, then squashing in after her, sitting sideways to give her as much room as possible. 'I'll breathe in when you breathe out and we should be okay,' he said, and she laughed. Such a good sound.

The vet was unlocking the door as they arrived, and Dante translated while Geli assisted him until his nurse arrived and they were no longer needed. Then they retired to the freezing waiting room.

'This is going to take a while,' she said, her breath a misty cloud. 'You should get back to your report.'

'It will keep.' He settled in the corner of the battered sofa and opened his jacket in invitation but she hesitated. Despite the last hour, she wasn't likely to forget the appalling way he'd behaved when she came up to his office. Okay, she'd been flirting a little but he should not have risen to it. Should not have kissed her, touched her and, when she'd responded with an eagerness that had wiped everything but need from his mind, he should not have rejected her.

He was a mess, he knew it, but the room was freezing and she wasn't going anywhere until she knew whether the cat was going to survive.

'Come on. You're shivering,' he said and, after what felt like for ever, she surrendered to the reality of the situation and sat down primly beside him. 'Snuggle up. You're letting out all the warmth,' he said, looping his arm around her and drawing her close, wrapping his coat around her.

She looked at him. 'Snuggle?'

'My mother used to say that. That's right, isn't it?'

'Yes.' She nodded and relaxed into him. 'My mother used to say that when we piled on the sofa to watch a movie on the television.'

'What movies did you watch together?'

'*Beauty and the Beast. Mary Poppins. The Jungle Book. White Fang...* We used an entire box of tissues between us when we watched that one.'

'Did White Fang die?' he asked, in an attempt to distract himself from the way her body was pressed against his, the tickle of her hair against his cheek.

'No, it was the scene where the boy had to send the wolf away for its own safety. He pretended he didn't love it any more. It was heartbreaking.'

'I can imagine.' He looked down at her. Or, rather, the top of her head. 'Is the cat going to make it, do you think?'

'It's hard to say. She seems to have taken a glancing blow from a car. There's a lot of superficial damage, cuts and scrapes and a broken bone or two.' She turned her head and looked up at him and, despite his best intentions, it took all his strength not to kiss her again. 'It depends what internal damage has been done.'

'Yes, of course.' *Look away. Think about the cat.* 'How on earth did she manage to get under the fence and drag herself back across the site?'

'Cats are amazing and she's a mother. Her babies needed her.'

'They survived without her.'

Her face pressed against the collar of Dante's shirt, his neck, sharing his warmth, Geli heard a world of hurt in those few words.

'Only because I found Rattino and you put up

that notice,' she said. 'Do you see your mother, Dante?'

He stared straight ahead and for a moment she didn't think he was going to answer her, but then he shrugged. 'Occasionally. She remarried, started a new family.'

'So you were able to return to Italy.'

'Just for the holidays. I was at school in England. Then I was away at university.'

'England or Italy?'

'Scotland. Then the US.'

Distancing himself from a father who was too busy with the new woman in his life to put him first, she thought. And from a mother who had found someone new to love and made a second family where he probably felt like a spare part...

She felt a bit like that, too, now that her sisters were married. It was no longer the three of them against the world.

'What did you read? At uni?' she asked. Anything to take away the bleakness in those dark eyes.

'Politics, philosophy and economics at St Andrews. Business management at Harvard.'

'St Andrews,' she repeated, with a teasing Scottish accent. 'And Harvard?'

He looked down at her, a smile creating a sunburst of creases around his eyes. 'Are you suggesting that I'm a little over-qualified to run a café?'

She made a performance of a shrug. 'What are you going to do with your degree except work as a researcher for a Member of Parliament? But business management at Harvard seems a little over the top. Unless you're planning world domination in the jazz café market?'

'Not ice cream and definitely not jazz cafés,' he said. 'The plan was that I gain some experience with companies in the United States before joining my father.'

'The fourth generation to run Vettori SpA?'

'Until Via Pepone got in the way.'

'Do you regret taking a stand?' she asked.

'Wrong question, Angel. The question is whether, given the same choices, I would do it again.'

'Would you?' she asked, shivering against him, not with the cold, where the snow had melted into her skirt and clung wetly to her legs, but at the thought of the boy who'd had his life torn apart, bouncing between adults who thought only of themselves.

'Maybe I was never meant to be the CEO of a big company,' he said, taking out his cellphone and thumbing in a text with the hand he didn't have around her shoulders. 'I hoped it would bring us closer together, but my father and I are very different. He thinks I'm soft, sentimental, trying to hang onto a past that is long gone. Incapable of holding onto a woman like Valentina Mazzolini.'

'When what you're actually trying to do is make a future for a place that you love.' A place where, sitting in Nonnina Rosa's kitchen as a boy, watching her cook, he'd been happy. Where he'd spent time as a youth on those long school holidays while his mother and father had been absorbed in new partnerships...

Isola was his home.

'Local politics seems to be calling me,' he admitted. 'There's no money in it, no A-list parties, just a lot of hard work, but maybe, in twenty or thirty years, if I've managed to hold back the march of the skyscraper and secure the spirit of old Isola in a modern world, they'll elect me mayor.'

'Tell me about Isola,' she urged. 'About your vision.'

'Vision?'

'Isn't that what the report you're writing is all about? Not just facts and figures, but your vision, your passion. The human scale?'

'That's the idea,' he said, 'but it's difficult to put all that into words that a politician can use. They need the facts and figures. It's dull stuff.'

'We're going to be here for a while and the only alternative is a pile of dog-eared Italian gossip magazines about people I've never heard of.' And she could have listened to Dante Vettori read the telephone directory. 'Go for it.'

'Go for it?'

'Tell me your plan, Dan.' He laughed—not some big ha-ha-ha laugh, it was no more than a sound on his breath, but it was the genuine article. 'Tell me why you love it so much,' she urged.

'It's real,' he said. 'This was a working class district with a strong sense of community. The park was closed and, with no green space, we made our own on a strip of abandoned land by the railway. The factories and the foundry are gone now, but people are still making things here because it's what they do, who they are. You know that, Angel. It's why you came.'

'Nothing stands still. There has to be change. Growth.'

'But you don't have to tear everything down. If they could just see—' He dismissed the thought with a gesture.

'What would you show them?' she pressed.

'The life, the music, the people.' And, at her urging, he poured out his love of Isola, his vision of the future.

'I don't think they'll wait twenty years,' she said when he fell silent. 'I think, given the chance, they'd elect you now.'

That raised one of his heart-stopping smiles. 'Maybe I should ask you to be my campaign manager.'

'Maybe you should.'

Their words hung in the air, full of possibilities, but she knew he hadn't meant it. It was just one of those things that slipped out when your mouth was working faster than your brain…

A tap on the outside door released them.

'I hope that's not another emergency.'

Dante didn't reply, but slipped out of his jacket and wrapped it around her while he went to investigate. He returned a few moments later with two carry-out drinks from Café Rosa and a box containing a pizza the size of a cartwheel.

'I didn't eat the supper you brought up,' he said, staring at the magazines for a moment before pushing them aside and opening the box to release the scent of tomatoes, cheese, basil. 'And you didn't get your break. It's a Margherita,' he added, glancing at her. 'No meat.' He checked the cups. 'This is yours. Hot chocolate.'

'*Posso abbracciarti,* Dante?' His only response was a frown. 'Did I mess that up?'

'That depends if you intended to ask if you could give me a hug.'

'You sent out for hot chocolate and my favourite pizza,' she pointed out. 'What do you think?' Then, grabbing a slice to cover her embarrassment, 'Don't fret. I was speaking metaphorically.'

'Metaphorically? Right.' Did he sound disappointed? She didn't dare look. 'Your Italian is coming along in leaps and bounds.'

'I'm memorising the phrasebook that Sorrel gave me.'

'Your sister?'

'The one who's married to an explorer.'

'And that was in it?'

'They've apparently moved on a bit since "my

postilion was struck by lightning".' She took a bite of the pizza and groaned with pleasure.

'But they haven't got to grips with the meta-phorical.'

She caught a trailing dribble of cheese with her finger and guided it into her mouth. 'It's a very small phrasebook.'

'Small but dangerous. Not everyone will get the subtleties of meaning.'

'Marco?' she suggested. 'He wasn't very sub-tle.'

'Nor was Roberto.'

'Oh, I've got him covered.' She adopted a pose. *'Non m'interessa*—I'm not interested. *Mi lasci in pace*—Leave me alone. *Smetta d'infastidirmi!*—Stop bothering me!'

'I take it all back. It is a most excellent phrase-book.'

'And this is the most excellent pizza. You texted Lisa?'

'I knew she'd worry when we didn't come back. And I thought you would welcome some warm food.'

'You thought right,' she said, helping herself to a second slice. Then she drank her chocolate, checked the time.

'Put your feet up,' Dante urged and, rather than unlace her boots, she picked up a magazine, placed it on the sofa and rested them on that. Then she eased the damp skirt away from her legs, tucked her feet up under her coat and invited him back into his jacket. He slipped his arms in and she leaned back against him as if it was the most natural thing in the world and, warm from the food, tired from what had been a very long day, she closed her eyes.

Dante watched with the envy of the insomniac as Angelica closed her eyes and was instantly asleep. Watched her as the silence grew deep around him and he closed his own eyes.

'Dante...'

He felt a touch to his shoulder and looked up to find the vet standing over him. He'd slept?

'It's over, Dante. She's in recovery.'

'The prognosis?'

'Fair. Cats are tough. We'll keep her here for a day or two and see how she does but, all things being equal, you can take her home in a couple of days.'

'Actually, she's a stray.'

'Good try,' he said, 'but she's going to need warmth, good food and care if she's going to make a full recovery. Tell the young lady that she saved her life. Another hour or two...' His gesture suggested that it would have been touch and go. 'You can see her if you want.'

'I'm sure she'll want to.'

'Come on through. Is there a spare slice of pizza?'

'It'll be cold.'

'My food usually is,' he said, helping himself to a slice and taking a bite.

'How much do I owe you?'

'My receptionist will send you a bill at the end of the month but I'll bring my family to the café at the weekend and you can give us all lunch. A small repayment for disturbing my evening.'

'My pleasure.'

Angelica stirred, opened her eyes, looked blank for a moment and then sat up in a rush as she saw the vet walking away with a slice of pizza in his hand. 'What's happened? How is she?'

'She's fine. We can take her home in a couple of days. Do you want to see her?'

'Please.' She stood up, picked up the magazine to return to the table and saw the front cover. An older man and a much younger woman arriving at some gala event. She didn't need to read Italian or check the names to know who they were.

He was Dante, twenty-five years on, just as she'd imagined him, with a touch of silver at the temple to lend gravitas. The woman, gold-blonde with ice-blue eyes, was wearing a designer gown that was a shade darker than her eyes and a Queen's ransom in diamonds.

He turned back to see what was keeping her and saw the magazine in her hand. He walked back to her and took it from her.

'The first time I saw her was at a party my father threw to welcome me to Vettori SpA. They were standing together but I was too self-absorbed to realise that he was in love with her. Even later, when he married her, I thought...'

'You thought he'd done it to hurt you.'

'Lisa told you that.' He shook his head. 'I was wrong. If I'd just taken a moment to look at him instead of her.' He looked bleak, utterly wretched and, unable to bear it, she touched his arm so that he looked up at her instead of the picture. 'He stood back and let me walk away with her.'

'Because he loved you both.'

'Maybe, but he chose her.'

Rejecting him for the second time. And yet

Dante had called him tonight, asked him for help. For her.

Before she could think of the words to tell him that she knew how much it must have cost him, he tossed the magazine back on the pile at the end of the table. 'Shall we go and see how cat number four is doing?'

They went through to the recovery area where she was sleeping off the anaesthetic. Large patches of fur had been shaved off. There were stitches, her leg was in a cast and she'd lost most of her tail.

'She looks like Frankenstein's cat,' he said.

'It's temporary. She's been through the mill and she'll need a lot of TLC, but one day, when her fur has grown back and the pain has retreated, she'll smell a mouse or see a bird and, without thinking, she'll be up and away, purring with pleasure at being alive and on the hunt.'

He was very still beside her, not speaking, not moving. Then he said, 'My father took Valentina away and married her secretly in Las Vegas. No one knew about it for months.'

'Well, that makes sense. The gossip magazines would have gone to town. Paps following you around, hoping for some reaction. Speculation about whether you'd been invited to the wedding. Whether you'd show.'

He managed a wry smile. 'I suppose I should be grateful. In the end, their extended honeymoon was brought to an end when Valentina's grand-mother died. The fact that she was very obviously pregnant made the front page of *Celebrità*.'

'That must have been a shock. Were you there? At the funeral?'

'No. My father sent me an email telling me that they were married, about the baby, asking me to stay away and I've done that.'

'Until tonight.'

He nodded.

'And he answered.'

'I imagine he's been waiting for my call.' He took out his gloves and pulled them on. 'When he realised that all I wanted was to get into the site to rescue a cat he was so relieved that he couldn't do enough.'

'Maybe he'll call you next.'

'If he doesn't, I'll call him.' He'd sounded mat-ter-of-fact as he'd talked about what had hap-pened but, when he turned to her, his normally expressive face was blank of all emotion. 'Shall we go?'

She paused on the step and, hunting for a way to change the subject, she looked up at the night sky. 'There are no stars.'

'It's the light pollution from the city.' Dante took her arm as her foot slipped on the freezing pavement. 'You have to go up into the mountains to see them.'

'In the snow? That would be magic.'

He looked down at her, his lips pulled into an unexpected smile. 'Would you like to go?'

Her heart squeezed in her chest. 'Now?'

'You're the advocate of seizing the day,' he reminded her. 'The forecast this evening suggested a warm front was coming in from the south. It could be raining tomorrow.'

For a dizzying moment she saw herself lying back in the snow, making angels with Dante, while all around them the world was sparkling-white, velvet-black and filled with diamonds...

This was why she'd come to Italy. For excitement, for moments like this. Her mother would grab the moment without a backward glance, without a thought for the consequences.

But she wasn't her mother.

'I have to check the kittens,' she said, sounding exactly like her responsible big sister, Elle. Elle who, just eighteen and with a college place waiting, had sacrificed her ambitions to stay at home and take a minimum-wage job so that she could feed her siblings, take care of her mentally fragile grandmother. Nurturing, caring, always there.

'Of course you do. And I have no confidence in the weather forecast. Experience suggests that we're going to be freezing for a while yet.'

They walked in silence for a while, their boots crunching against the frozen snow, their breath mingling in the bitter air, but Dante had offered her something special and she wanted to give him something in return. Something that would show him that she had not been rejecting him.

Something personal, something that she would only share with someone she— Someone she trusted.

'It's blonde,' she said.

'Blonde?' He glanced down at her.

'You wanted to know the natural colour of my hair. It's white-blonde.'

'Really?'

'I have to dye my brows and lashes or they'd be invisible. There must have been a Scandinavian roustabout with the Fair the year before I was born.'

'I can't imagine you as a blonde,' he said.

No, well, she'd seen the quality of blonde he was used to dating. 'I did once consider leaving a natural streak,' she said. 'For dramatic effect.'

'*Cara*...you are all the drama a man can take.'

'Is that a compliment? No, it's not... Anyway,' she said, rapidly moving on, 'Great-Uncle Basil said I'd look more like Lily Munster than Morticia Addams so that was that.'

'You are like no one, Angel. You are individual. Unique.'

Unique? 'Not exactly the kind of compliment a woman queues up to hear but I'll take it.'

'You don't need me to tell you that you're stunning, Angelica Amery. You have Roberto and Gennaro and Nic and Marco lining up to turn your head.' She laughed and he drew her closer to his side.

The café was closed when they arrived back and they went in the back way.

At the first landing Dante stopped. 'Go and tell the kittens that their *mamma* will be home soon. Have a warm bath. I've got a few things to do.'

'Do you ever sleep, Dante?'

'Not much,' he admitted.

'Not enough,' she said, lifting her cold hands

to his face and smoothing her thumbs across the hollows under his eyes. 'You need to quieten your mind before you go to bed.'

The world stilled. 'How do I do that?' he asked.

'First you switch off your computer. Then you write a list of the things you have to do tomorrow so that you don't stay awake trying to remember them.'

'But I've turned off my computer,' he reminded her. 'How do I do that?'

'Use a notepad and a pen.'

'That's a bit old school.'

'Maybe, but that's the rule.'

'Okay, pen, paper, list. Then what?'

'You take a bath—don't have the water too hot; your body needs to be cool to sleep.'

He leaned against his office door, folded his arms. 'Go on.'

'Sprinkle a few drops of lavender oil on your pillow before you get into bed and, when you close your eyes, think about all the good things that happened to you today.'

'Good things? What do you suggest? Our trip to the police station? That I've been lumbered with two more kittens and their injured mother? Spent hours in a freezing—'

'Don't be such a grouch. You helped a stranger who was in a fix. Rescued a cat that would have died without you doing something big, something difficult. You spoke to your father.'

She rubbed her hand over his arm, a gesture of comfort to let him know that she was aware how hard it must have been to ask him for help.

He looked at her hand, small, white, with perfect crimson-tipped nails, lying against his shabby worn waxed jacket sleeve, and for a moment he couldn't think about anything but reaching out and wrapping his arms around her, just holding her.

'Think about how good that pizza tasted.'

He looked up, realised that she was looking at him with concern. He straightened, breaking the contact. 'Is that it?'

'No. Last thing of all, you should think about all the good things you're going to do tomorrow so that you wake up happy.'

'Is that more of your mother's wisdom?'

'Yes...' Her eyes sparkled a little too brightly. 'Can I give you that hug now, Dante?'

'A metaphorical one?'

'Actually, I think you deserve the real thing,'

she said, stepping close and, before he could move, she'd wrapped her arms around him, her cheek was against his chest. 'You have been a one hundred per cent good guy today, Dante Vettori. Think about that.'

Dante closed his eyes and inhaled the scent of this woman who had blown into his life like a force of nature.

She smelled of pizza and chocolate, there was a hint of antiseptic where she'd washed after handling the cat. And something more that he was coming to recognise as indefinably his Angel...

'You can hug back,' she murmured after a moment. 'It doesn't hurt.'

How could she be so sure? How could you want something so much and dread it at the same time? But ever since she'd asked him to hug her while they were waiting for the vet, leaning against him as she'd put her feet up, he'd been thinking about how it would feel to really hold her, to kiss her, live for the moment. What would happen if he followed through on those kisses without any thought of the past or the future?

Selfish thoughts. Dangerous thoughts. But if anyone deserved a hug it was Angelica and he tightened his arms about her, holding her close for a long perfect minute, but she was wrong about it not hurting. It hurt like hell when, after a while, she pulled away.

CHAPTER NINE

'If you licked the sunset, it would taste like Neapolitan ice cream.'
—from *Rosie's Little Book of Ice Cream*

GELI STOOD AT the top of the stairs hugging her arms around her, holding in how it felt to have Dante's arms around her. Not in some crazy mad moment when one or both of them had temporarily lost control, but the kind of hug you'd give a friend in a shared moment. Special, real…

He was special. She could not imagine how hard it must have been for him to call his father and ask for his help but he'd done it for her. Okay, he'd done it for the cat, but if it hadn't been for her he wouldn't have been out there in the freezing night looking for a stray cat in the first place.

He *was* special and she would be his friend and if that was all he could give then she'd ask for nothing more.

* * *

Dante watched as Angelica ran up to the top floor to check on her precious kittens then went into his office and sat down at his desk. He'd left his laptop on and the screensaver was drifting across the screen waiting for him to touch a key and continue with his dry, full of facts report that, despite all the promises and encouragement from the minister, would be filed and forgotten.

He turned the machine off, pulled a legal pad close, uncapped a pen and wrote the number one in the margin.

Quieten his mind. Make a list…

It began easily enough as he jotted down half a dozen of the most urgent things he had to do in the coming week. He added a note of something to include in his report. Crossed that through. Wrote: *vision*, *passion*… He underlined the last two words. What was it Angelica had asked him? *'What would you show them?'*

The life, the music but, above all, the people. Not some slick documentary film but real people talking straight into the camera, telling those who would tear this place down what was so great about it. Why they should think again.

He sent a text to Lisa, wishing them both *buon*

viaggia, buona fortuna, so she'd see it when she
woke. He hoped he'd done the right thing. That
Lisa and Giovanni's love would heal the rift between their families. If it did they would have
Angelica's crazy arrival to thank for that.

Angelica—

She had never had a father, had lost her mother
at a pitifully early age. She might wear the pro-
tective black she'd hidden behind as a child but
on the inside her world was richly coloured and
filled with wonderful memories. Tragedy, need,
had not shattered her family; it had bound it together.

She'd asked him if he saw his mother and
he'd implied that she hadn't had time for him.
The truth was that he'd been so angry that she'd
found someone else—had *looked* for someone
else when he'd sacrificed his world to stay with
her—that he'd walked away. He could hear Angelica telling him that he should be grateful that
his mother had been strong enough to look forward, move on. Be grateful for the small half-
sisters she and her husband had given him and
reach out to make them part of his world.

This evening, when he'd called his father to
ask for a favour, they'd spoken as if they were

strangers and yet assistance had arrived within minutes. Angelica had assumed guilt, but all he'd heard was the fear of a man with his head buried in the sand.

He looked at the phone lying beside the pad, then picked it up, flicked through the photographs, staring at one he'd downloaded from *Celebrità* for a long time before he sighed, thumbed in a text to let his father know that they'd found the cat, adding his thanks for his prompt response. There was more, but some things had to be said face to face. He added his initial and pressed send then, with the phone still in his hand, he texted his mother to let her know that he'd call her in the morning.

He tapped the end of the pen on the pad for a moment, added one final item to his list and then went upstairs.

The apartment was quiet. The kittens were curled up together in the shelter of their box. And, hanging from the knob of his bedroom door, was a small linen drawstring bag with a hand-embroidered spray of purple lavender. It contained a little glass phial with a handwritten label—*lavender oil* and a date—and a note.

*Gloria—as in Knickerbocker Gloria of ice
cream fame—produces this from her own
garden. It's a bit magic, but then she's a bit
of a witch.*

*I've done with the bathroom so use the
tub—a shower will only wake you up.*

Dormi bene. Sogui dolci. G.

Sleep well. Sweet dreams.

The café did not open on Sunday and Geli got up
early to the sound of bells ringing across the city,
fed the kittens, gathered cleaning stuff from the
utility room and, with a sustaining mug of tea,
went down to her workroom.

Dante had cleared out everything but her boxes
and she set to work cleaning everything thoroughly before setting up her work tables and
drawing board, putting together her stool. Her
corkboard was hung and was waiting for the
scraps of cloth, pictures—anything and everything that would inspire her.

Three hours later, everything was unpacked,
her sewing machines tested, her Mac up and
running and all the boxes flattened and neatly
stacked away in the corner, ready to be reused

when she found somewhere of her own. Not that she could hope to find somewhere as perfect as this.

It was a fabulous space, and she took a series of pictures on her phone which she sent to her sisters, attached to an email explaining that there had been a problem with the apartment she'd rented but that she had found temporary accommodation and everything was great. She might even make a snowman later.

Elle replied, asking for a picture of the snowman.

Sorrel wanted to know: *what problem?* And actually her sister was probably just the person to fight her battle with the bank if things got sticky. She'd chase them up on Monday.

Right now she just itched to sit at her drawing board and begin working on an idea for a design that had been forming in her head ever since she'd seen those black beads in the market. Dusty, hungry; it would have to wait until she'd had a shower and something more substantial than a pastry for breakfast.

She was heading for the bathroom when Dante, dishevelled and wearing only a robe, emerged from his room and her heart jumped as if hit by an electric current.

'Angel—' He was sleep-confused, barely awake, giving her a moment to catch her breath. Gather herself. 'What time is it?'

'*Buongiorno*, Dante,' she said with what, considering the way her heart was banging away, was a pretty good stab at cool amusement. 'Did you sleep through your alarm?'

He dragged a hand through his hair and his robe gaped to expose a deep V of golden skin from his throat to his waist, the faint spatter of dark hair across his chest. Releasing the knee-weakening scent of warm skin.

'I don't have an alarm clock,' he said, leaning against the door frame as if standing up was still a work in progress, regarding her from beneath heavy lids. 'I don't need one.'

'No?' She knew what the time was, but raised her wrist and pointedly checked her watch. 'You intended to sleep until ten o'clock?'

'Ten? *Dio*, that lavender stuff is lethal.'

It wasn't just the lavender that was lethal. Wearing nothing but a carelessly tied robe, Dante Vettori was a danger not just to her heart, her head, but to just about every other part of her anatomy that was clamouring for attention... 'You had a late night,' she reminded him.

'So did you but it doesn't appear to have slowed you down.' He reached out and she twitched nervously as he picked a cobweb from her hair. 'What on earth have you been doing?'

'Giving the storeroom a good clear-out.' Forcing herself to break eye contact, she brushed a smear of dust from her shoulder. 'I wanted to set up my stuff so that I can start work.' She should move but the message didn't seem to be getting past the putty in her knees. 'Give me ten minutes to clean up and I'll make breakfast.'

'Ten minutes.' He retreated, closing the door, and she slumped against the wall. A woman should have some kind of warning before being confronted with so much unfettered male gorgeousness.

Really.

She had just about got some stiffeners in her knees when he opened the door again. 'I took your advice and made a list,' he said.

He had? 'Good for you. Clearly, it helped.'

'That's to be seen. One item concerns you.'

'Oh?'

'You won't be moving.'

'I won't?' Her heart racketed around her chest. He wanted her to stay... And then reality kicked in. 'Did Lisa change her mind about taking Giovanni to the wedding?' she asked, concerned.

'No. They should be safely on their way by now.'

'Well, that's good. For them,' she added in case he thought her only worry was about having somewhere to live.

'Let's hope so but, in the meantime, you're going to be here all day, working a shift or on your designs and you can't keep rushing across town to look after an injured cat and a bunch of kittens.'

'It's a kindle,' she said. 'The collective noun. It's a kindle of kittens, a clowder of cats. Would it be necessary to move them? As you said, I'll be around in the day and you'll be here in the evening, at night.'

'Not all the time. I've had my head stuck in this damned report when I need to be out there, drumming up support. Making a noise. I'll be going to Rome some time this week. And I've decided to supplement the report with a DVD.'

'A picture says a thousand words?'

'That's the idea. I thought I'd put together a

short film. There'll be library footage of people at last summer's jazz festival, the collective lunches at the *giardino condiviso*, the "green" construction projects and the creation of the street art.'

'That's a start but you'll need people. Interesting faces, characters.'

'Two minds with but a single thought… I'll intersperse the clips with people talking about why they love this place. Not just the old guys who've been here for ever, but the young people who are drawn here. You, for instance.'

'Me?'

'You're so excited about it. And, as Lisa said, you're good for business.'

'Oh, I see. I'm going to be the hot totty that keeps the old guys watching.'

'Not just the old guys.' He straightened. 'Anyway, that's for next week. I was talking about the cats and it's going to be easier if you stay here and I move into Lisa's flat.'

'You…?' According to Lisa, the heating was on a thermostat, a cheap timer switch would turn the lights on and off and, in any case, she was going to have to go and feed the goldfish and check that everything was okay while he was away. 'Is that really necessary?'

'Cara...' He lifted a hand and, although his fingertips barely brushed her cheek, her body's leaping response was all the answer she needed. Of course it was necessary. She would be here, in his space, all day, all evening, either in the café or working on her designs.

He'd made no attempt to deny the frisson of heat, the desire that simmered whenever they were in the same room, but he'd made it clear in every way that, despite the attraction between them, he was still mourning the woman who'd abandoned him.

He might be mourning for Valentina, but right now he was there, leaning against the doorframe, arms folded and very much awake beneath those slumberous lids as he called her *'cara'* in that sexy, chocolate-smooth accent.

She'd probably be doing him a favour if she reached out, tugged on the tie that was struggling to hold his robe together, pushing him over the edge so that he could blame her for his 'fall'.

She wouldn't have to push very hard. He wanted it as much as she did and she had him at a disadvantage. Once her hands were on his warm satiny skin, his resistance would hit the floor faster than his robe and neither of them would be thinking about anything except getting naked. But afterwards he'd feel guilty, there would be awkwardness and she didn't just want his body, luscious as it was. She was greedy. She wanted all of Dante Vettori.

'Are you sure you'll be able to handle the goldfish?' she asked, stepping back from the danger zone.

'Are you mocking me, Signora Amery?'

'Heaven forbid, Signor Vettori.'

She was mocking herself. She'd come to Isola looking for artistic and emotional freedom. Marco, gorgeously flirtatious, would have been perfect for the kind of sex without strings relationship she had envisaged. Or even the elegant Gennaro. Throwing Dante Vettori in her path on day one was Fate's cruel little joke.

'Now, if you'll excuse me, I have a litter tray to clean.'

Dante shut the door and leaned back against it. He'd made his list then soaked in a tub, filled with water that was not too hot, in a bathroom still steamy and scented with something herby that Angelica had used. Sprinkled a few drops of lavender oil on his pillow before lying back and recalling all the good things that had happened that day. He'd implied it would be hard but a dozen moments had crowded in…

The moment he'd walked into the café that morning, seen Angelica and experienced the same heart-stopping response as the night before. Watching her laugh. Avoiding her eyes as every male in the *commissariato* had paid court to her, knowing that they would be laughing just for him. The weight of her body against his as she'd slept while the vet operated on their stray…

And then he'd thought about all the good things he'd do today so that he'd wake up happy.

He'd have breakfast with Angelica. Bounce ideas off her, about his film. He'd call the vet for an update on the cat because she'd be anxious. Afterwards, they could go into the city for lunch and he'd show her the Duomo, wander through the Quadrilatero so that she could window-shop at the great fashion houses. Finally, supper in front of the fire. And bed. With her? Without her?

He'd have woken very happy if, when he'd opened his eyes, she had been lying beside him, her silky black hair spread across the pillow, her vivid mouth an invitation to kiss her awake…

He tightened his hand in an attempt to obliterate the peachy feel of her skin against his fingertips, the soft flush that warmed her cheeks, darkened her eyes, betraying her, even while she attempted to distance herself with words. They both knew that all he had to do was reach out to her and she would be in his arms.

It had been there from the moment he'd looked around and their eyes had met; in that first irresistible kiss. Romantics called it love at first sight, but it was no more than chemistry bypassing ten thousand years of civilisation, sparking the atavistic drive in all animals to procreate. A recognition that said, *This one. This female will bear strong children, protect your genes...*

That was how it had been with Valentina. She'd been at the party thrown to welcome him home, welcome him into the Vettori fold. She was there when he'd arrived, standing with his father, a golden, glittering prize, and he'd been felled by the metaphorical Stone Age club.

He was still suffering from the after-effects of the concussion and, whatever Lisa advised, whatever the temptation—and he'd been sorely tempted—he would not use Angelica as therapy.

Before he could weaken, he took a bag from his wardrobe, packed everything he was likely to need in the next week and then took a wake-up shower. An espresso, a quick run-through of the heating system and he'd be gone.

And then he opened his bedroom door and the smell of cooking stopped him in his tracks.

'An English breakfast,' he said, dropping his bag in the hall and walking into the kitchen. 'That takes me back to those first days when my mother rented a house in Wimbledon. Sunday mornings and everyone walking their dogs on the Common.'

'Pastries for breakfast are all very well,' Angelica said without turning around, 'but a long day should start with something more substantial.'

'I noticed that you'd bought oatmeal.'

'Oatmeal is for weekdays. Sunday demands *il uovo strapazzato, la pancetta e il pane tostado*.'

'You've been at that phrasebook again.'

'I've moved on to food and drink. Sadly, I can't offer you *la marmellata*. I forgot to buy a jar when I was in the shop.'

'Eggs, bacon and toast with marmalade? Really? I thought you were looking for new experiences, not clinging to the old.'

'So you don't want any of this?' she asked, looking back over her shoulder as she waved a wooden spoon over the scrambled eggs, crisp thin bacon.

'Did I say that?'

Her mouth widened in a teasing grin. 'That's what I thought. You can make the coffee while I dish up. Then you can tell me all about this ice cream parlour you want me to design.'

She was brisk, businesslike, keeping her distance, which should have made their enforced intimacy easier to handle. It didn't. 'You're eager to start?' he asked, concentrating on the espresso but intensely aware of her standing a few feet away.

'I imagine you want it to be open in time for the spring?' She turned to him, a frown buckling the clear space between her lovely brows. 'Or was it just something you said to shut me up about paying rent?'

'No...' He shrugged. 'Maybe. I didn't want an argument, or rent complicating the accounts, but I do have a room that isn't earning its keep and the more I think about it the more the idea grows on me. We'll take a look after breakfast if you've got time.'

Breakfast...

On the intimacy level, that word rang every bell.

* * *

'This is it.' Dante stood back and Geli stepped into a large square room with French windows that opened out onto a snow-covered courtyard. He'd warned her that the heating wouldn't be on and she was glad of a long cardigan that fell below her hips and the scarf she'd looped around her neck. 'What do you think?'

With an injured cat to nurse and three lively kittens to look after, an ice cream parlour to design, an inconvenient lust for a man who was locked in the past and snow, Geli thought that this was so not why she'd come to Italy.

She walked across to the window and looked out. There was the skeleton of a tree and a frosted scramble of bare vines on the walls that promised green shade in the summer. An assortment of tables, chairs and a small staged area in the corner were hidden beneath a thick coating of snow, undisturbed by anything other than a confused bird, floundering in an unexpectedly soft landing.

Dante joined her at the window. 'It looks bleak on a day like this but in the summer—'

'I can see,' she said.

The snow would melt, the vines would flower,

the kittens would be found good homes and designing an ice cream parlour would be a small price to pay for a temporary workspace. She'd find somewhere to live and Dante... Maybe her heart would stop jumping every time she saw him, every time he came near.

Meanwhile, there was this very tired room to bring to life.

She drew a rough square on the pad she was carrying and then fed out a tape measure. 'Will you give me a hand measuring up?'

He took the end and held it while she read off the basic dimensions—length, width, height of the room. She made a note and then added detailed measurements of the positions of doors, windows, lighting and electrical sockets.

'Have you any thoughts on a colour scheme?' she asked.

'Anything but pink?' he volunteered.

'Good start,' she said. 'I thought we might carry through the dark green from the café. It will tie the two parts together and look cool in the summer. I'll add splashes of colour that we'll carry through to the courtyard with pots filled with flowering plants.'

'That's very different to the designs you showed me. Rather more sophisticated.'

'You're right. I see a space and I get carried away with my own ideas of how it should look.'

'But?'

She shrugged. 'This is a sophisticated venue. If I was doing this in a UK high street I'd be using bright colours to catch the eye. I'd want nine-teen-fifties American cars, a vintage soda fountain and a jukebox with fifties-era records, but you have live music and Italy has a fabulous car industry,' she said as she gathered her stuff and headed for the door.

'Keep the jukebox. We can turn it off when there's live music.'

'Okay, but you need to think about who is actually going to use this space. Who do you want to attract? Young people looking for somewhere to hang out? I doubt ice cream and fifties pop is going to do it. Most of our sit-down customers in the UK are young teenage girls, families—birth-day parties for kids do really well—and women meeting up for a chat over a treat.'

'And the stand-up ones?'

'That's the takeaway trade.'

'Of course.'

'Having second thoughts?'

'No…I can see a daytime and early evening market for this, but you're right. It needs to fit in with what's going on outside.'

'You'd better give me some idea of your budget. Are you thinking Ferrari or Fiat 500?'

'I hadn't given it much thought.'

She grinned. 'My ideal client.'

'Show me what you've got and I'll have a better idea of what it's likely to cost,' he said, heading back to the rear lobby where he'd left his bags.

'The major capital expenses will be the freezer counter for the ices, jukebox and, depending on the look you want, furniture.' She looked around, already seeing it on a summer evening with the doors thrown open, musicians on the stage. 'There'll undoubtedly be some rewiring needed, the floor will need sanding and refinishing and whatever wall treatment you decide on.'

'I'm going to have to sell an awful lot of ice cream to pay for that.'

'I'll draw this up on my CAD program today and put together some ideas for you to look at.'

'Great. Give me your pen.'

She gave it to him and he leaned in to jot something down on the corner of the pad she was holding. Too close—so close that she could see a single thread of silver in amongst the glossy dark hair.

'This is my email address...' He looked up, catching her staring. 'Send me your ideas. It'll be light relief from the politics. Is there anything else?'

Yes... 'No.'

He nodded. 'I'll leave you in peace, then.'

About as much chance of that as a hen laying a square egg, she thought. He might have slept like a log but she'd tossed and turned all night. Getting up had been a relief.

'You've got my number. Give me a call if you have any problems,' he said as he shrugged into his heavy jacket, found his gloves in the pockets, continued searching... Swore softly under his breath. 'I left my scarf at the vet's office.'

The soft, very expensive scarlet cashmere scarf that he'd wrapped around the injured cat. The kind that usually came gift-wrapped, with love, at Christmas... Not this last Christmas, she suspected, but the one before.

As he turned up his collar she took off her own scarf and draped it around his neck. 'Here. This will hold you.'

He opened his mouth as if to say something, clearly thought better of it and left it at, 'Thanks.' Then concentrated on tucking in the scarf and fastening the flap across his collar. 'I'll ring the vet later. To ask about the cat,' he added.

'I usually switch my phone off when I'm working, but you can leave a voicemail.'

'Angel…'

'Yes?'

'You know how to set the alarm? The kitchen staff will turn it off when they arrive.'

'Lisa took me through it. Matteo is in charge while she's away. I start at seven for the morning shift,' she added, 'and work until everyone goes home when I'm on the evening shift.'

'He'll probably close up early. Once people get home they won't come out in this.'

'Very wise of them, if not great for business.' He didn't move. 'Will you come in for breakfast?'

'If I have time.'

'How about if I suggest chef puts porridge on the menu as a cold weather special? With fruit, cream, a drizzle of honey and, to give it a little Italian panache, a dash of Marsala to keep you warm while you're out doing your Zeffirelli thing.'

'Hold that thought.' He reached for the door handle and, still holding it, said, 'Will you be in it? The film. It was your idea.'

'It was?'

'You said, "What would you show them?"'

'So I did.' She lifted her shoulders in an awkward little shrug. 'If it will help. Do you want me in English or Italian?'

'Either. Both. Whatever comes out. Nothing polished or rehearsed. Just you.'

She managed a wry smile. 'I think I can guarantee that. You'll need an editor to pull it together.'

'I don't want a slick tourist promo. I'm looking for something raw, something from the street.'

'Why don't you use a student? Does the university have a media school?'

'Another great idea.'

'I'm full of them,' she said and, since he didn't seem in any hurry, 'for instance, do you have any contacts in local television?' He seemed thrown by the question. 'An historic part of the city struggling to retain its identity?' she prompted. 'It's the sort of thing that would get airtime in the early evening magazine programmes at home.'

'I suppose so.' He did not sound enthusiastic and she didn't press it.

'Okay, what about the local press? And social media? Politicians use it to target supporters and make themselves look good, but it's a two-way street. You can target them. Put your film on YouTube, post a link on their Facebook page and Twitter account and get everyone involved to share, leave comments, retweet.' He was still looking at her as if she had two heads and she shrugged. 'I did all the early promo for Rosie, our ice cream van, and I learned a lot. Mostly about how desperate the media are for stories that will fill airtime and the big empty spaces in their pages.'

'I'm sorry. You're right, of course. I'll give it some thought.'

For a moment neither of them said anything.

'Angel...'

'Dante...'

'What?' he asked.

'You should go. The goldfish will be getting lonely.' Hungry... She meant hungry...

CHAPTER TEN

'Forget science. Put your trust in ice cream.'
—from *Rosie's Little Book of Ice Cream*

DANTE SLUNG HIS bag and laptop case on the passenger seat of his car. Then he undid the neck flap of his jacket and touched the scarf that Angelica had placed around his neck.

He had other scarves, and had been about to say so, but this one was warm from her body and as she'd draped it around his neck he'd caught that subtle scent that seemed to stay with him whenever he touched her. He stood in the cold garage, lifted it to his nose, breathed in, but it was nothing he could name—it was just Angelica.

And it made him smile.

Geli settled at her computer, called up the CAD program, put in the dimensions of the room then began to play with ideas, searching through her boxes for fabrics and colours to create mood boards.

Dante called and left a voicemail to let her know that Mamma Cat was recovering and that he'd pick her up first thing on Monday.

When she found herself picking up her phone and, like some needy teenager, listening to the message for the tenth time, she deleted it and drove herself crazy trying to find the right combination of words—in Italian—that would bring up freezer counters and jukeboxes. Something her phrasebook was singularly useless at providing. It would be the perfect excuse to call Dante, but she told herself not to be feeble and eventually she got it and printed out photographs of the ones that inspired her schemes.

That night she tried her own remedy, listing all the good things that had happened that day and could only come up with one. Dante had touched her... And that wasn't good. At all.

'I'll take over here,' Matteo said as she began to make yet another espresso. 'Dante's taken the cat upstairs and he wants to know what to do with her.'

'Oh, right. I won't be long.'

She took off her apron and took the stairs two at a time. A cat carrier had been left in the kitchen but there was no sign of Dante. No doubt he was picking up something he needed from his room.

She took a breath, knelt down to look through the grille at the cat. 'Oh, poor lovely. Shall I take you to see your babies?'

'The vet sent antibiotics,' Dante said. She looked up. He was wearing a dark suit, silk tie, a long elegant overcoat and looked, no doubt, like the man who'd been destined to run the family business. All it needed was a red cashmere scarf to complete the image. Instead, he had the black one, hand-knitted by her grandmother, draped around his neck. 'One tablet in the morning until they're gone. She's had today's dose.'

'I'll take care of her. You're going to Rome now?'

'I've got a taxi waiting. Will you take the carry basket back to the vet?'

'Of course.'

'You'll need your scarf,' he said.

'No,' she said, her hand on his to stop him as he began to unwind it. 'It's freezing out there and I have others.'

'If you're sure. Thank you.' He reached in his

pocket, took out a key and placed it on the kitchen table. 'Here's the spare key to Lisa's place. The lights are on a timer switch and I've set the heating to run continuously on low, but the goldfish will get lonely.'

'I'll take care of him. Go... *Arrivederci! Buon viaggia!*'

He smiled again, touched her cheek lightly with the back of his fingers. *'Arrivederci, cara.* Take care.'

Cara...

It meant nothing. Italians used it all the time. The market traders, the waiters, the customers all called her that.

It was only when she was watching Mamma Cat, purring as her babies rubbed against her, that she realised what he'd said.

The goldfish will get lonely...

There was no more snow but the temperature remained below freezing. While daytime business was brisk, with everyone looking for hot food and drinks to keep them going, Dante was right; once they were home nothing was going to tempt them out again.

Geli worked the early morning shift when there

was a rush for espresso and pastry, but finished at nine, leaving the rest of the day to the regular staff, who were short of evening tips. The money would have been useful but she nagged the bank and, with no distractions, she got an awful lot done. She hardly had any time to think about Dante.

Okay, she thought about him when he surprised her with a text to let her know he'd arrived safely and a photograph of a frosty Coliseum to show her that Rome was freezing, too.

Obviously, she replied—it would be rude not to—and in return sent him a photograph of Mamma Cat, recovered enough to give her kittens a thorough wash.

She couldn't help thinking of how brilliant he'd been about the cat when she dropped off the carry basket and paid the vet's bill using her credit card, despite the receptionist's insistence that she'd send a bill at the end of the month. It was wince-making but there was no way she was letting Dante pay it.

She thought of him later, too, when the vet's nurse called at the café on her way home with a bag containing his scarf, stiff with blood and mud, and was disappointed to discover that she was not going to be able to hand it over in person.

Shame she didn't bother to wash it, Geli thought sourly, but it had simply been an excuse to see Dante. The scarf was ruined.

She gave him the bad news the next day, when she emailed him photographs of the mood boards she'd prepared for three different schemes for his ice cream parlour and colour-wash impressions of what each of them would look like.

The first was a full-on US fifties-style diner, with booths and a jukebox and hot rods. In the second she replaced the booths and paid tribute to Milan with ultra-modern furniture and an artwork motif of sleek Italian cars. For the third she used her own vision of the room. Dark green walls, the mix-and-match furniture painted white and a sparkly red jukebox. She suggested shelf units for the walls, with bright jars of toppings and blown-up details of ice cream sundaes on the walls and, through the open French windows, a glimpse of planters overflowing with flowers. It was the simplest, least expensive and, in her opinion, would be the most adaptable.

He responded instantly.

You're right. Let's go with number three. D.

She smiled, and replied.

You have excellent taste. How are the meetings going? G.

It was only polite to ask.

Slowly. Important men make a point of keeping you waiting so that you'll understand how generous they are in sparing you five minutes of their valuable time. D.

He didn't mention the scarf.

They're all too busy sending tweets and posting pictures of themselves doing good works on Facebook to waste time on real people. Social media is the way to go. G.

And she attached a picture of Lisa's goldfish, peering at her out of the bowl, to which she added a speech bubble so that he appeared to be saying, 'Tweet me!'

She went to the Tuesday market and bought more beads from Livia for a project and looked at some wonderfully soft cashmere yarn in the same clear bright scarlet as the scarf that had been ruined. She passed over it and picked up half a dozen balls in a dark crimson that exactly matched the colour of her nails.

Dante, clearly bored out of his skin hanging around waiting to talk to people, sent her a text asking how the cat was doing. She took a photograph of Mamma Cat looking particularly Frankensteinish and then she opened a new page on her Facebook account that she called *A Kindle of Kittens.*

She posted snippets of the story, pictures of the kittens and then the one of Mamma Cat. Then she added a speech bubble to the photograph of Mamma Cat, saying, 'Like me on Facebook' and sent it to Dante with the link.

He immediately 'liked' the page and left a comment.

I'll keep the black one. D.

The black one? Was he making some kind of veiled reference to her? She shook her head and replied.

She's all yours.

The icon on his post was for Café Rosa's Facebook page and when she checked it out she discovered that it was simply a listing of the musicians who would be appearing and the artists who were exhibiting there with some of their work. Nothing personal.

Elle and Sorrel sent her identical texts.

Who is D?

She replied:

He's my landlord and my boss. Why didn't you warn me that it would be freezing here?

She sent Dante a text, asking him how he was sleeping.

I've been making a list, remembering the things I've done, thinking about what I'm going to do the next day. It's not working. D.

That's politics for you. Concentrate on the small pleasures. Every life needs ice cream. G.

And thinking about him was unavoidable when she curled up on the sofa in the evening with her headphones on as she worked on her Italian and knitted his scarf, her head against a cushion that smelled faintly of the shampoo he used.

Fortunately, there were distractions.

She had called in at a fashion co-operative where local designers displayed high quality one-off pieces, and designs that could be produced in small quantities for boutiques. She wasn't sure if they would accept work from a non-Italian, but she was living and working in Isola and that, apparently, was enough. She'd worn her coat and had photographs of other pieces on her phone and she'd been invited to bring along a finished piece for consideration.

Of course, she'd had to tell Dante and he'd been thrilled for her.

Marco came in every day, still hoping that she'd change her mind about spending the evening with him. He was charming, good-looking and she knew she was mad not to get out for a few hours, try and get Dante out of her head, but he wasn't the man to do it. She wasn't sure if such a man existed.

Dante laughed at a video Angelica had posted on the kittens' Facebook page of one of the kittens chasing a strand of wool and falling asleep mid-pounce. It earned him a stern look from the Minister's secretary. She was right. It wasn't funny.

He could hear Angelica saying, 'Pull it, pull it...' and the rumble of a man's laughter in the background.

Who was pulling the wool? Marco, Nic, Gennaro...?

He told himself that he had no right to care. But he did. He cared a lot.

He'd been cooling his heels in a dozen offices since he'd arrived, been given a dozen empty promises and he'd scarcely noticed. The only thing he'd cared about were the texts from Angelica. The photographs she sent him.

A selfie of her with Livia, and a stack of beads she'd bought. A bowl of porridge lavishly embellished with fruit, honey and cream. Some balls of wool she was using to knit him a scarf to replace the one that had been ruined. He'd seen Nonnina knitting and he knew that every inch of the yarn would have been touched by her as it slid through her fingers...

She hadn't said one word about the kitten-botherer.

He put the phone away and stood up. 'Please

give the Minister my apologies,' he said, picking up his laptop bag and heading for the door.

'You're leaving?' she asked, startled. 'But you have an appointment with the Minister.'

'I had an appointment with the Minister over an hour ago and now I have to be somewhere else.'

'But—'

'I'll tweet him.'

He stood on the steps of the Ministry, breathing in the icy air as he pulled on his gloves, wrapped Angelica's scarf around his neck.

He'd spent four days chasing his tail in Rome, waiting for people to see him and getting nowhere. No surprise there. He'd known how it would be and yet he'd come anyway.

Wasting his time.

Running away from what had to be done. Running away from his feelings for Angelica Amery.

On Thursday evening, Geli settled down with her headphones on, working on her Italian while she added a few more inches to the scarf.

Listen then repeat...

Buongiorno. Desidera?

'*Buongiorno. Desidera?*'

*Buongiorna. Mi dà uno shampoo per capelli
normali per piacere.*

*'Buongiorna. Mi dà uno shampoo per capelli
normali per piacere.'*

Si, ecco. Abbiamo questo...

Geli heard another sound over the lesson and
lifted one ear of the headphones. Someone was
at the door. She checked her watch. They'd be
clearing up downstairs and this would be Matteo
bringing her some little 'leftover' treat.

She switched off her iPod, stuck her needles in
the wool and went to open the door and the smile
of welcome froze on her face.

It was the same every time—no, not the same;
this time it was worse. Or did she mean better?
The heart kick, putty knees and a whole load of
X-rated symptoms were getting a lot of practice.

'Dante... You're back,' she said stupidly.

'Despite the best efforts of the airline and the
weather to keep me in Rome for another night,'
he said. 'I waylaid Matteo on his way up here
with this,' he went on, indicating the small tray
he was holding. Not coming in, despite the fact
that she'd stood back to give him room. 'Is there
something I should know?'

'Know?' For a moment she didn't understand what he meant. Then the penny dropped. Did he think that she and Matteo…? Shocked that he could believe her so fickle—and just a bit thrilled—make that a whole lot thrilled—that he actually cared—she managed a puzzled frown. 'Didn't you ask him to come up and check that I was okay every night before he went home? Bring me up a little treat? What is it?' she asked, reaching for the cover. 'Chef was making cheese-cake—'

'No,' he said, moving it out of her reach.

She looked up. 'It's not cheesecake?'

'It's chocolate truffle tart. And no, I did not ask him to come up here bothering you.'

He did! He thought that she was encouraging Matteo and he was not amused. Considering that he'd made it plain more than once that he wasn't interested—okay, they both knew that he was in-terested, but he wouldn't, couldn't do anything about it—his attitude was a bit rich, but it still gave her a warm, fuzzy feeling that wasn't help-ing the knee problem one bit.

'He wasn't bothering me,' she said, leaving him standing on the doorstep. 'On the contrary,' she called back as she headed for the kitchen, leaving him to follow in his own good time. 'I'm assuming there's enough of that tart for two?'

She took a couple of cake forks from the cutlery drawer then, as she heard the tray hit the kitchen table, she stretched up to take two plates from the rack. Before she could reach them, Dante caught her wrist and turned her to face him.

'Was it Matteo pulling the wool?'

She didn't pretend not to know what he was talking about, but met his gaze head-on. 'You didn't have to fly back from Rome to ask me that,' she pointed out, quite rationally, she thought, considering that she was backed against the work surface, that the front of his overcoat was pressed very firmly against her sweater. That his breath was warm against her cheek. That his hand had slid from her wrist and his fingers and hers were somehow entangled… 'You could have just sent a text.'

His fingers tightened over hers. 'What would you have replied?' he demanded, his eyes darkened with an intensity that might have scared her if it hadn't been making her heart sing. He cared…

'I'd have replied that Matteo brings me cake every evening as an excuse to play with the kittens.'

'The kittens?' he repeated, confused. 'Why would anyone even notice the kittens when you're here?'

She leaned into him to hide a smile too wide to fit through a barn door.

'He's besotted with them.'

'The man's a fool.'

'No… He's going to take one, maybe even two of them, when they're old enough to leave their mother.'

'Not the black one.' His face softened as he looked down at her. And this time there was no doubt about his meaning. 'Not Mole.'

'Molly. She's a girl.' Her legs were trembling. 'I told you, Dante. She's all yours.' And then, because she had to say something to break the tension, 'Do you like chocolate tart?'

'I like this.' He took the forks from her, placed them on the work surface behind her, took her face between his hands, brushed his lips over hers. 'I've been thinking about this.'

'This' was a kiss, angled perfectly to capture her mouth. Tender, thoughtful, tasting lips, tongue, nothing hurried or snatched, he bombarded her senses with a flood of heat until, like the city bells on Sunday morning, they were clamouring for attention. Screaming, *Nooooo...* as he drew back a little to look at her.

'I've been thinking about you, Angelica Amery, and all the good things I'm going to do with you.'

Okay, enough with the talking—

She reached for the buttons of his overcoat but he put his hand over hers, stopping her, and she looked up. 'You have too many clothes on.'

'Not for where we're going.'

What? 'I don't—'

'This is date night,' he said. 'I've called for you at your door and I'm going to take you stargazing. We'll also eat, talk and, at some point during the evening, I'll undoubtedly hold your hand.'

'Just my hand?'

'It's our first date. Your rules.'

'No. I was just—'

He touched his finger to her lips to stop her saying that she was just... Actually, she didn't know what she was 'just' doing. Mouthing off that all men saw when they looked at her was an opportunity for sex? A bit hypocritical when the

whole idea of old-fashioned commitment terrified the wits out of her.

His hand moved to her cheek. 'It's not just
about sex, Angel.'

She swallowed. 'It's not?'

He could read her mind now? She'd thought
she had a problem when she'd discovered that
her apartment didn't exist, that her money was
gone, but this was trouble on a whole new level.

This wasn't about mere stuff. This was about
taking the biggest risk imaginable.

'No.' His hand cradled her cheek, his touch
warming her to her toes as he looked straight into
her eyes. 'I've learned that the hard way. There
has to be more if a partnership is going to clear
the hurdles that life throws in your way. Survive
the knocks.'

'That's a heck of a lot to put on a first date,
Dante.'

'I know, but if you don't start out with the highest expectations it's always going to be a com-
promise. Are you okay with that?'

Was she? He'd been totally honest with her from
the beginning and she'd tried to be the same. She
hadn't been coy, hadn't tried to hide the way she
felt whenever she was within touching distance

of him. But this was exposing the soft nerve tissue, the stuff that hurt when you poked it.

'You want the truth?'

'*Parla come magni, cara.* Speak as you eat. I have always told you the truth,' he reminded her.

'I remember,' she said. 'Even when it hurt.'

'Even when it hurt,' he agreed, easing back a fraction, as if preparing for bad news, and the bad news was that she wanted to grab him, hold him close.

'The truth is that it scares the pants off me. The metaphorical pants,' she added quickly, trying to keep this light.

He didn't smile. 'Do you want to tell me why?'

'I've spent my entire life losing people. My father, half of everything I am, was gone before the stick turned blue—unknown, unknowable. No name, no picture, just an empty space.'

'Your mother didn't tell you anything about him?'

She shook her head. 'And when she was there it didn't matter. She filled our lives, Dante, and I never thought about it, about him, but when she died—'

He put his arms around her, drew her close.

'You realised you would never know. That you'd lost not just one but both your parents.'

'Then along came Martin Crayshaw—obviously not his real name—and for a while he was everything a storybook father should be until, having stripped us clean, stolen our lives, he disappeared without so much as goodbye.'

'Did the police ever catch up with him?'

'My grandmother was in a state of nervous collapse and Elle, my oldest sister, was only just eighteen. She was afraid that if the authorities discovered what had happened Sorrel and I would be taken into care.'

'She didn't report it?' She shook her head. 'How is your grandmother now? You are very close, I think.'

'Better. Much better. Great-Uncle Basil's arrival has given her something I never could. He takes wonderful care of her now. They are the dearest of friends.'

'And your sisters fell in love, got married, have families of their own.'

'I'm happy for them. They married wonderful men and I love my nieces and nephews to bits, but it's as if I've been left behind.'

'No, Angel. They haven't left you behind;

they've simply moved on to the next stage in their lives.' His lips brushed her hair. 'Relationships change. When my mother made a new life for herself, started a new family, I was so angry...'

'Angry?' she repeated, surprised. 'I can't imagine that.'

'One of the things I put on that list you said I should make was to call her.'

She leaned back a little so that she could see his face. 'Did you?'

'We had a long talk. Cleared away a lot of the dead wood. I've been doing a lot of that.'

'So that there's room for fresh new growth.'

'I knew you'd understand.' He caught her hair between his fingers and pushed it back so that she couldn't hide behind it. 'I told her all about you and your lists. About that moment when I first saw you, the front of your coat plastered with snow and looking exactly like the princess in a fairy tale book she used to read to me when I was little. About Rattino's unscheduled appearance. That made her laugh. She wished she'd been there to see it.'

'Hmm, I suspect it's one of those experiences that improves with the rose-tinted spectacles of time.'

'The sort of thing you tell your grandchildren when they ask how you met.'

Grandchildren? This was their first date...

'And I told her that you were knitting me a scarf to replace the one she sent me at Christmas because it was ruined when we rescued Ratty's mother.'

'Your mother gave you that scarf?'

'Yes…' She saw the moment when he realised what she'd actually thought. 'Did you imagine that I would wear something that Valentina had given me?'

'I… It was a beautiful scarf,' she said.

'Yes, it was.'

'Now I feel really bad. Maybe I could have rescued it if I'd tried harder, but I have to confess that I really enjoyed putting it in the rubbish.'

He roared with laughter. 'My mother said that you sounded like a keeper.'

'She doesn't know me, Dante. You barely know me.'

'It's been a steep learning curve,' he admitted, 'but so far I like everything I've seen.'

'Ditto,' she said, pleased, awkward. 'I'm glad you talked to her.'

'I have you to thank for that,' he said, 'and I'll

tell you something—the hardest part was picking up the phone.'

'Are you saying that I need to pick up the metaphorical phone?'

'It's just a date, Angel.'

She shook her head. 'No, it's not,' she said. They both knew it was a lot more than that. 'We're both trailing baggage. We should both probably start with something less intense.'

'I'm doing my best here.'

'It's not working but, given the choice between staying here and knitting a scarf or having you hold my hand while we look at the stars—'

'The stars have it?'

She shook her head. 'You had me at holding hands. The stars are a bonus.'

'In that case, I think we'd better get out of here before my good intentions hit the skids. You need to go and wrap up in something warm. I'll go and put Matteo out of his misery and tell him that he's got overtime babysitting the kittens.'

CHAPTER ELEVEN

'Love is an ice cream sundae with all the marvellous toppings. Sex is the cherry on top.'

—from *Rosie's Little Book of Ice Cream*

THEY WERE BOTH unusually quiet as Dante drove out of the city. He was, presumably, concentrating on the traffic—driving in Italy was not to be taken lightly—while she was absorbed in the change in their relationship. Wondering what had happened in Rome...

Then Geli, sneaking a glance at his profile, lit only by the glow from the dashboard, discovered that Dante was doing the same and practically melted in her seat.

'Where are we going?'

He returned his full attention to the road. 'Does it matter?'

'No. The only thing that matters is that I'm going there with you.'

And in the darkness he reached across and took her hand, holding it lightly until he slowed to turn off the highway and they began to climb into the mountains.

After a while, the lights of a village appeared above them but, before they reached it, he turned off and pulled onto an area that had been levelled as a viewing point.

'Wait...' Dante came round, opened the door and helped her from the car, keeping her arm in his as they walked to the barrier and looked out over the valley.

There was no moon, but the Milky Way, so thick that it was hard to make out individual stars, silvered the flat dark surface of a lake far below them.

'What lake is that?' she asked. 'I know Como is the nearest but there don't seem to be enough lights.'

'No, that's Largo D'Idro.' He glanced at her. 'It's the highest of the lakes but very small. There are no tourist boats doing the rounds of celebrity villas because there are no celebrities. It's popular for water sports.'

'But not in this weather. There's snow right

down to the shore. I thought the lakes had a famously mild climate?'

'Nowhere is mild in February,' he assured her, 'and the lakes have been known to freeze over in severe winters.'

'They don't tell you that in the tourist brochures.'

'Maybe that's because we like to keep it to ourselves. There's something rather magical about sitting in a steaming hot tub when the air temperature is below freezing.'

She gave him a thoughtful look. 'Is that what you have in mind?'

'On our first proper date?' He took her hand and held it. 'You will be escorted to your front door and maybe, if I'm lucky, you'll have enjoyed yourself enough to risk a second one.'

Geli thought that she was more than ready for an improper date; that hot tub sounded like a lot of fun. But she had complained that men never asked women out on dates any more and, while she wasn't totally convinced that he was going to kiss her on the cheek and say goodnight at the door, she would go along with it.

'In that case, if we're going to act like kids, it's time to make snow angels.' She looked around, caught his hand and, tugging him after her, headed towards a gently sloping area of untouched snow. 'The stars will look even better if we're lying down.'

She flung herself down into the snow, laughing as she swept her arms and legs wide to make an angel while Dante looked on.

'If you don't get down here and join in I'm going to feel stupid,' she warned. 'You are also blocking out the stars.'

'I just love watching you.'

Geli stilled.

'What happened to you in Rome, Dante?'

'Nothing happened. Everything happened. For months my head has been filled with the past, the mess we all made of it. While I was in Rome all I thought about was you. How much I enjoyed getting your emails and texts. How much I wished you were there with me.'

'And yet you're standing up there and I'm down here.' She held out her hand. 'I promise you, this is a lot more fun if you join in.'

He took it and then lay beside her in the snow. About to tell him that the magic only happened when you made your angel, she pressed her lips together. He had missed her. Now they were lying together in the snow, looking up at the stars and Dante Vettori was holding her hand. That was all the magic she could handle right now.

'Do you know the constellations?' she asked.

'Some of them...'

They lay there in the snow pointing out the stars they recognised until the cold drove them in search of warmth, food and they drove up to the ski resort where, in a restaurant lively with an après ski crowd, they shared an *antipasti* of grilled vegetables and a *risotto alla pescatora*, rich with prawns, squid and clams.

As they finished their meal with ice cream and espresso, Geli said, 'No meat and nothing to drink. I'm a tough date.'

'I don't drink and drive, I didn't have to have the grilled vegetables and I would have chosen the risotto even if I'd been on my own. Are you free tomorrow?'

'The dating rules say that I shouldn't be that easy,' she said. 'I'm going to sound desperately sad and needy if I say yes.'

'I'm doing the asking so that makes two of us, but this isn't something we can do next week. I have an invitation from one of the big fashion houses to their pre Fashion Week party. It's tomorrow,' he said, 'or you're going to have to wait until the autumn and hope I'm still on their party list.'

'You're kidding me?' Milan Fashion Week was as big as it got. Invitations to parties thrown by the designers were like gold dust.

'They probably think I'm my father. Dante, Daniele... What are you doing?' he asked.

'Just checking that my chin isn't down there on the floor,' she said. 'Do you think he'll be feeling slighted? Your father?'

'He won't notice. Valentina presents a local evening television show so she gets invited to everything.'

'Oh... I had no idea.'

'Lisa didn't tell you?'

'No. She started to talk about her but I said that you had already told me what happened and she got the message.' But it explained his reluctance to contact local TV about his film. 'Will Valentina be there? With your father?'

'More than likely, but this is not about them. I'm asking you. Would you like to go as my plus one?' And then Dante told her who the invitation was from and she nearly passed out with shock.

Her mouth was moving but nothing was coming out and she fanned herself with one hand while indicating that she'd be with him in a moment with the other. He caught the fanning hand, said, 'I'll take that as a yes.'

'No—'

'No?' He sounded genuinely shocked, as well he might.

'You don't have to put yourself through this for me.'

'She's married to my father, Angel. If he and I are going to have any kind of relationship we have to move on. But you're right. Maybe what I'm asking...' He linked his fingers through hers. 'Will you do this for me?'

'You want me to be your wing man?'

'Above and behind me? No, my angel, I want you beside me all the way.' And he leaned across the table and kissed her.

His lips tasted of coffee and pistachio ice cream and, like every kiss they'd shared, it was all too brief. She'd waited long enough...

'Dante—' He waited. 'You do realise that this isn't actually our first date?'

'It isn't?'

'Don't you remember? When you insisted on taking me to the *commissariato*—'

'I certainly remember that. I hope there wasn't an emergency while you were there because no one would have heard the phone.'

She rolled her eyes. 'No, think… You said, "Is it a date?"'

'And you said yes.'

'Actually, I asked if it was "another" date. Made some stupid comment about going steady. We'd already made a date to sit up late one night and tell one another stories. I think we can quite legitimately count this as a two-in-one. A double date for two.'

'So you're saying—be patient with me, I don't want to get this wrong—that this is our third date?'

She just smiled and he raised a hand in the direction of a passing waiter. *'Il conto…'*

Dante opened his eyes, saw Angelica's dark hair spread across the pillow, her lovely mouth an invitation to kiss her awake and thought for a moment that he was dreaming.

He kissed her anyway and, like Sleeping Beauty, she opened her eyes, smiled, hooked her hand around his neck and drew him down to her so that she could kiss him back. A morning kiss, new as the dawn, as welcome as the spring.

'*Ciao, carissima,*' he said, his hand tracing the profile of her body as she turned towards him; the lovely curves he'd explored with such thoroughness during a night in which he'd been reborn. '*Come posse servirvi?*'

She frowned, mouthed the words then, her smile widening into soft laughter, she said, 'Did you really ask how you can serve me?'

'Would you like tea?' he asked, his hand lingering on her thigh. 'Or I could carry you to the shower and get creative with the soap. Or—' a blast of Abba's *Dancing Queen* shattered the silence '—*Dio!* What is that?'

'The alarm on my phone.' She rolled out of bed and he watched her walk, naked, to her bag, find her phone and turn it off. She looked back at him. 'Your service will have to wait, I'm afraid. I have to go to work.'

'Matteo is not expecting you. I told him that you had other plans today.'

'What? You can't do that.' He loved how shocked she was. How committed…

'I'm the boss. I can do what I like.'

'But it's market day. They'll—'

'They'll manage,' he said, peeling himself off the bed, wrapping his arms around her. 'Now, where were we, *mio amore*? Tea, shower—' he nuzzled the lovely curve of her neck '—or is there some other way I can serve you?'

She kissed his neck, ran her hand down his back. 'Why don't we start with the shower and see how it goes from there?'

Geli's hand was shaking as she called Elle. She hadn't the faintest clue what she was going to say to her; she only knew she had to hear that calm voice.

'Sorry, I can't talk right now. Leave a message and I'll call you back when whatever crisis I'm having is sorted.'

A message? Which one would that be? *I'm going to a swanky party thrown by one of the world's most famous fashion designers. I can't stand up because Dante Vettori spent the night melting my bones. I'm in love...*

No, no, no! It had been the most thrilling, tender, perfect sex, outshining anything she could have imagined in her wildest fantasy, but Dante was right, love was more than that.

It was lying together in the snow in a universe so quiet that you could hear a star fall. It was making the toughest phone call in the world in order to find a cat which might already be dead. It was small things, like texts that said nothing except I'm thinking of you.

'Just me,' she said. 'Nothing important, just looking for some big sister advice about what to wear to a bit of a do. Love to everyone. Catch up soon.'

Clothes... Concentrate on clothes.

She was standing in front of her wardrobe when Dante returned from Lisa's flat. 'You were an age. Was there a problem?'

'You could say that. The goldfish was floating on the top of the tank. I've been at the pet shop trying to find a match.'

'Any luck?'

'We found one with similar markings. It's a bit bigger, but with any luck Lisa will put that down to a growth spurt.'

'And if she doesn't?'

'You'll just have to own up.'

'Thanks for that.' She turned back to the wardrobe and the two dresses hanging over the doors. 'Have you heard from her since she arrived?'

'Just a text to let me know that she arrived safely. What are you doing?'

'I'm trying to decide which dress to wear tonight. The black or the burgundy-red.'

'So nothing taxing, then.' She gave him what Elle called 'the look'. 'Obviously, you'll wear the black but you'll look fabulous whatever you wear, *cara*. Meanwhile, I have something important to say. I need you to concentrate.'

Heart in her mouth, she turned to him. 'What is it?'

'It's this. *Posso baciarti, carissima?*'

'Testing my Italian, *carissimo?*' she asked, raising her arms and looping them around his neck. *'Voglio baciare si...'*

His answer was a long slow kiss, followed by an intimate lesson in advanced Italian.

It was the accessories that finally settled the matter of what she would wear. Her black dress had been refashioned from a fine jersey vintage dress that she'd found in a trunk in the attic.

The sleeves had been cut in one with the dress and she had narrowed them below the elbow.

The neck was a simple V, cut low, but merely hinting at her breasts and she'd used a series of darts to bring it in at the waist. Worn as it was, it was timelessly elegant. Tonight, she'd cinched it in with an eight-inch-wide basque-style black suede and silver kid belt that was fastened at an angle by a series of small diamanté buckles.

When she was finally satisfied that every detail was perfect, she picked up a tiny silver and black suede clutch and her long black velvet evening coat and went through to the living room.

Dante, looking jaw-droppingly handsome in a tux, was standing in front of the fire, one hand on the mantel, the other holding a glass, his face burnished by the flames as he gazed into some dark abyss. Then, as he lifted the glass, he saw her and it never made it to his mouth.

'Angel...' He put down the glass, crossed to her, took the coat from her, holding onto one of her hands. 'Pretty gloves,' he said, admiring the fingerless black lace mitts she was wearing. 'I want to kiss you but you look so perfect.'

She lifted her hand so that he could kiss her fingers and he took his time about it, kissing each one in turn before turning her hand over and kissing her palm.

'What a gentleman,' she said, laughing, to disguise the fact that she was practically melting on the spot, and tapped her cheek. 'You can't do much damage there.'

He touched his lips to the spot.

'Or there.'

She lifted her chin so that he could kiss her neck, by which time he'd got the idea and continued a trail of soft kisses along the edge of the neckline of her dress. When he reached the lowest part of the V he slid his hand beneath the cloth and pushed it aside, then audibly caught his breath as he realised that she wasn't wearing anything underneath it. *'Mia amore...'*

He settled her silver and jet necklace back into place, carefully removed his hands, stepped back and held out her coat. As she turned and slipped her arms into the sleeves, he said, 'Have you grown?'

She hitched up her skirt a few inches to reveal the slender steel vertiginous heels of her intricately laced black suede boots.

He studied them for a moment, then her belt,

then he looked up and smiled. 'I am so going to enjoy undressing you when we get home.'

By the time the limo approached the red carpet, Geli was shaking with nerves. 'All the women will be wearing designer dresses, diamonds,' she said.

'You *are* wearing a designer dress. And every one of those women will wish they were wearing that belt.'

'You think so?'

'Believe me. They'll know that every man in the room will be wishing he was the one unfastening those pretty buckles tonight.'

'Now I'm blushing.'

'Then it's just as well I'll be the only man in the room who knows for sure what you're not wearing tonight.' It was probably as well that the car stopped at that moment. Dante climbed out, offered her his hand, said, 'Big smile, Angel...' and she stepped out of the car to a blaze of flashlights from the army of paparazzi waiting for the celebrities.

The room was like a palace in a very grown-up fairy tale: everything beautiful, everything perfectly arranged, a stage set for exquisitely dressed

players who moved in a circle around the legend-
ary central character who was their host, and she
watched, fascinated, as the famous—Hollywood
stars, supermodels—paid court.

Dante introduced her to some people he knew,
she drank a little champagne, ate a little caviar
and wished she hadn't. He went to fetch her a
glass of water and, as she turned, searching the
crowd for a sight of Valentina or his father, she
came face to face with the Maestro himself.

'*Signora...*'

'Maestro. *Piacere... Mi chiamo* Angelica
Amery. *Sono Inglese.* My Italian is not good.'

'Welcome, Angelica Amery,' he said, switch-
ing to English. 'It's always a pleasure to meet a
beautiful woman, especially one with so much
courage.'

'Courage?'

'I believe that, including the waitresses, you are
the only woman in the room not wearing a dress
designed by me. This vogue for vintage clothes
will put us all out of business.'

'*Mi dispiace,* Maestro, but I could not afford
one of your gowns or even the one I'm wearing
for that matter. This belonged to my great-grandmother.'

'She was a woman of great style, as are you, *cara*. And I adore your belt. The asymmetrical slant of the buckles complements the era of the dress so well. Where did you find it?'

'*Grazie*, Maestro. I designed it myself. I was inspired by an Indian bracelet I saw on the Internet.'

'Quite perfect.' He nodded, held out his hand before moving on and when she took it he raised it to his lips. 'Come and see me next month. We will talk about your future.'

'*Grazie*...' But he was already talking to someone else and, when she looked down, she realised that he'd tucked his card under her lace mitten.

He'd given her his card. Asked her to come and see him. He'd said her belt was 'quite perfect'...

She stood for a moment trying to breathe, trying to take in what had just happened and then spun round, searching for Dante so that she could tell him.

Taller than most in the room, he should be easy to spot, even in this crush, and after a moment she spotted his broad shoulders jutting from a small alcove. He had his back to her but, as she took a step in his direction, she saw who he was talking to.

Valentina Vettori was older than she'd realised, older than Dante, but even more beautiful in the flesh than in her photograph despite, or perhaps because, her eyes were brimming with tears.

It was like watching a car crash you were unable to prevent. The way she reached for him, the way he took her into his arms and held her while her tears seeped into the shoulder of his jacket. And all the joy of the last twenty-four hours, the triumph of the evening, turned to ashes in her mouth.

Valentina had been his lover—he'd grieved for her loss for over a year.

He'd only known her for a week.

Look away, she told herself. *Look away now...*

It was a moment of the most intense privacy and no one in the celebrity-hunting crowd had noticed. No one cared but her.

As she dragged her eyes from the scene in the alcove she saw someone else she recognised. Make that no one but her and Daniele Vettori who, glass in hand, was looking around, clearly wondering where his wife had got to.

'Signor Vettori,' she said, walking towards him, hand outstretched. 'I am so glad to meet you. I wanted to thank you for your help the other night.' His smile was puzzled but he turned to look at her. '*Sono* Angelica Amery,' she said. 'The crazy cat lady.'

'Signora Amery… *Piacere.*' He took her hand. 'I did not realise that you were English. You are here with Dante?' He sounded surprised. Looked hopeful.

'I'm a dress designer—in a very small way,' she added. 'Dante thought I might enjoy this.'

'And are you?'

'Very much.' Until two minutes ago she had been on top of the world. 'Is your wife with you?' she asked as his eyes wandered in search of her. Anything to keep him focused on her.

'She's here somewhere, making up for lost time networking. We were very late. Alberto—our son—wouldn't settle. We have a nanny but Valentina… I'm sorry; you do not want to talk about babies.' He smiled, gave her his full attention. 'Where is my son?'

'He's gone to find me a glass of water. It's rather a crush.'

'Please, take this.' He offered her the glass he was holding. 'My wife is breastfeeding so she's avoiding the champagne.'

'Oh, but—'

His smile deepened and it was so much like his son's that a lump formed in her throat. 'There's a price to pay. You will have to stay and talk to me until Dante returns.'

'That's not an imposition, it's a pleasure.' She took the glass from him, hoping that her hand would not shake as she took a sip.

'Did you meet Dante in England, Signora Amery?'

'Please, everyone calls me Geli.'

Everyone except Dante...

'*Grazie*, Geli. *Mi chiamo*, Daniele.'

'Daniele... And, in answer to your question, no. I came to Isola to work. Dante helped me when I had a problem with my apartment.' She had to chase up the bank. She'd let things slide; there had been no urgency, but now—

'Angelica...' She physically jumped as Dante placed his hand on her shoulder, standing possessively close. He was paler and there was the faintest smear of make-up on the shoulder of his jacket that only someone who knew what to look for would see, but he had remembered her water. 'It appears that I'm redundant here.'

'Not at all.' She took the glass from him and handed it to his father. 'Daniele merely loaned me this glass until you returned. It was for Valentina but she seems to have disappeared.'

'I saw her a minute ago. I believe she was heading in the direction of the cloakroom.'

'Then I will wait here with you if I may,' Daniele said.

The two men looked at one another for a long intense moment before Dante put out his hand and said something in Italian that Geli did not understand. And then she was holding two glasses as the two men hugged one another.

And she was the one blinking back tears when Valentina found them, linked her arm in Daniele's and said something to her in Italian, speaking far too quickly for her to understand.

'Geli is English, *cara*,' Daniele said, taking the fresh glass from Dante and handing it to her. 'She is the heroine who searched my construction site in the snow and saved the injured cat.'

'*Alora*... Such drama. You are so brave...' Her expression was unreadable and she could have intended anything from genuine admiration—possibly for risking her nails—to veiled sarcasm. '*Come*... How is she? The cat?'

'She is healing fast and contented now that she is with her kittens,' Geli assured her.

'Then all is right with her world.' She looked at Dante and for a long moment it was as if she and Daniele were not there. Then she snapped on a smile and said, *'Dolci...'* before turning to her. 'Sweet... I do not know if you are aware but I present an early evening magazine programme on regional television. We are always looking for light stories. Good news. Maybe we could feature your cat and her kittens? Are they photogenic?'

Geli, astonished and not entirely sure what to make of her invitation, turned to Dante but, getting no help there, said, 'Well, Mamma Cat is a looking a bit like Frankenstein's monster at the moment, shaved patches and stitches, but the kittens more than make up for that.'

'Perfect. Will you do it? Obviously, the programme is in Italian, but I can translate for you or—' Geli waited for her to suggest that Dante came along to translate '—we could film them at home and I can do a voice-over.'

'Grazie, Valentina. I'm working on my Italian but it might be kinder to your viewers if you did the talking.' Valentina's smile was strained and, on an impulse, she began telling her about the drama of Rattino's appearance, giving it the full action treatment as she described Lisa's horror,

the women leaping on chairs, her diving under the table. By the end of the story they had gained a small audience and everyone was laughing.

'*Bravissima!*' Valentina clapped. 'That! I want that! We'll use subtitles. *I gattini*…where are they now?'

'They're in our apartment,' Dante told her. 'Why don't you come and see them? Come to lunch tomorrow, both of you. I have a gift for Alberto—' his father looked wary rather than pleased '—and I have a project that I'd like to discuss with Valentina.'

'Oh?'

'Angelica is an artist and we're making a film about the need to preserve the heart of Isola.'

'From people like me?'

'It isn't personal, Papà. It was never personal.'

There was another of those long looks, but after a moment his father nodded. They chatted for a few more minutes before Valentina spotted someone she had to talk to and the party broke up in a round of very Italian hugs. Only Geli saw that, while her husband was occupied with her, Valentina took the opportunity to whisper something in Dante's ear, saw his nod of acknowledgement, imperceptible to anyone who wasn't watching closely.

'Would you like to go on somewhere?' Dante asked as they climbed into their car.

'No. Thank you.'

'You can't know how glad I am you said that. Did you have a good time? I saw you talking to our host.'

'Did you? Actually, he was congratulating me on being the only woman present with the courage not to be wearing one of his gowns.'

'Amore...' he exclaimed. 'I never thought. I'm so sorry.'

'Why? It is what it is and when I explained that this dress had belonged to my great-grandmother he forgave me.'

'Are you serious?'

'That my dress is eighty years old or that he forgave me?'

'Madonna, mia! Either...both. Is it really that old?'

'My great-grandmother kept a ledger of her clothes. When she bought them, how much they cost, where she wore them. This one is by Mainbocher, the man who designed the dress Wallis Simpson wore when she married the Duke of

Windsor. Great-grandma didn't wear it after that. She disapproved of divorce, disapproved of the abdication...disapproved of pretty much everything, apparently, except beautiful clothes.'

She knew she was talking too much but Dante, it seemed, was disinclined to stop her. Maybe he was interested in vintage fashion...

'We have trunks full of clothes in the attic, not just hers, but my grandmother's too. She was a sixties dolly bird, a contemporary of Twiggy, but that's more Sorrel's era. Lucky for us that Elle had no idea of the value of vintage clothes when she was selling off the family silver to pay the creditors.'

Talking too much and all of them the wrong words.

'The dress is perfect, Angel. You were so busy looking at everyone else that you didn't notice that they were all looking at you.'

He reached across the back seat of the limo to take her hand but she pretended she hadn't noticed, lifting it out of his reach to check the safety of a long jet earring.

'The Maestro admired my belt, too,' she said. 'It's a Dark Angel original.'

'I hope you told him so.'

'I did… He kissed my hand, gave me his card and asked me to go and see him next month. When the shows are over.'

'I think that is what you call a result.'

'Beyond my wildest dreams,' she assured him. And maybe that was it. The jealous gods only let you have one dream at a time… 'And you, Dante? Did you accomplish everything you wanted tonight?'

He sighed, leaned back. 'Everything is not for mortal men,' he said, eerily reflecting her own thoughts, 'but as much as I could have hoped. The fact that you were already talking to my father made it a great deal easier.'

'Did it? You sounded rather cross.'

'No…' He shook his head. 'How did you come to be talking?'

'Oh, the usual way. You know how it is at parties. We were in the same space at the same time. I was looking for you so that I could tell you about meeting the Maestro. He was looking for his wife and about to see her crying into your shoulder so I distracted him by introducing myself as the crazy cat lady.'

'Then I'm not imagining the touch of chill in the air. Congratulations, Angelica. You have not only made a hit with the one man in Milan famously impossible to impress, but appear to have excelled yourself in diplomacy.'

'My sisters would be astonished on both counts,' she assured him. 'I usually say exactly what I think and hang the consequences.'

'I applaud your restraint but, since we're alone, feel free to share your thoughts with me.'

She closed her eyes. That was it? No explanation, no attempt at justification? No reason for her to forget what she'd seen and...no, she would never forget the tenderness with which he'd held Valentina. She knew how that felt and she wasn't in the mood to share.

'I'm thinking that you took me to the party as an excuse to see Valentina. That, sooner or later, she will leave your father and come back to you and he knows it.' When he still said nothing, made no attempt to deny it, she added, 'And I think that new goldfish will be nervous, all alone in a strange tank. You should keep him company tonight.'

CHAPTER TWELVE

*'Eat ice cream for a broken heart. It freezes
the heart and numbs the pain.'*
—from *Rosie's Little Book of Ice Cream*

DANTE TOLD THE driver to wait, walked Angelica
upstairs to the door of his apartment, unlocked it
and waited while she walked in, turned to him,
blocking the way.

'Angel—'

'Don't... Don't call me that.'

'I just wanted to thank you for everything you
did this evening. You were kinder than any of us
had a right to expect and we are all in your debt
for ever.'

'I didn't do it for you. I did it to spare your father's feelings.'

'I understand, but whatever you think you
saw...' He wanted to tell her that what she'd seen
was not what she imagined. She was right about
Valentina—he had thought that meeting her on

neutral ground with hundreds of other people present would be easier for both of them. He had been as wrong about that as Geli was about everything else. Valentina had almost fainted with shock when she'd seen him, had been desperate for reassurance that he wasn't about to blow her life apart.

Now he was the one clinging on, hoping that Angelica would remember that he'd respected her enough to be honest with her about Lisa's motives when he could have gone for the easy lie.

She'd been angry then, too, but not for long. She'd thought things through and accepted that he had been doing what was right.

All he could do was hope that, given time, she would understand that tonight—

'Hello, you're back early.' Matteo, slightly tousled, as if he'd been asleep, appeared from the living room. 'I thought you'd be going on somewhere.'

'It's been a long day,' he said. 'Any problems?'

'No.' He grinned stupidly. 'Actually, I've been talking to my mother. She's at home all day and she'd be really happy to take care of the cats. If it would help?'

Not in a million years. Right now, the only

thing anchoring Angelica in his life was the cats and they were going nowhere.

'We'll talk about it tomorrow. Go down and wait in the car. I'll give you a lift home.'

'Thanks. *Ciao*, Geli.' He grabbed his coat from the hook and thundered down the stairs.

When he had gone, Angelica opened her mouth as if to say something, but closed it again. Closed her eyes as if it was too painful to look at him. He felt the shock ripple through her as he cradled her face, wiping away the tears squeezed from beneath her lids with the pads of his thumbs, but she didn't pull away.

'Carissima...' Tears clung to her lashes as she opened her eyes. 'May I offer some words of wisdom from a woman it is my honour, my privilege to know?'

'Please, Dante,' she protested, but she was still there, the door open.

'Cherish the good things that happened to you this evening, hold them close. They do not come often.'

'I know...'

'Make a list of all the things that hurt you so that you won't lie awake turning them over in your head.' Her mouth softened a little as she recognised her own advice returned with interest and, encouraged, he continued, 'Take a bath, not too hot. Sprinkle a little lavender oil on your pillow and then, while you wait for sleep, think of all the good things that you will do tomorrow so that you'll wake happy.'

She swallowed. 'Good things?'

'The early shift in the café, flirting with Marco and all your other admirers.' She shrugged. 'The appointment with your client to finalise the scheme for his ice cream parlour.' She might move out, but she wouldn't walk away from a promise and it would keep her close. Give him hope.

'That's not in my diary.'

'It's in mine. Ten o'clock.'

Another shrug.

'And then lunch with—'

'You expect me to have lunch with you and... With all of you?'

'I believe, in fact I'm certain, that if you will talk to my father about our film he'll be more receptive.'

She frowned. 'Why would he listen to me?'

'Because you are a beautiful woman. My worst moment tonight was seeing you with him, watching him flirting with you. He has Valentina and yet he still cannot help himself.'

'Maybe he's protecting himself,' she said. 'Making an exit plan. Preparing to be left.'

'Something you'd know all about, *cara*?'

'What?' She shook her head. 'What are you talking about?'

'You told me yourself that you're scared to death to risk your heart, always holding something back, protecting yourself from hurt in case you're left behind by those you love. Wearing mourning black in case they die.'

She opened her mouth to protest, but nothing emerged.

'It isn't going to happen. Valentina will stay with him because he gives her everything she ever wanted.'

'Not you.'

'She was the one who left, *cara*. I would never have made her happy and she had the sense to know that. The courage to go after what she wanted.'

'Taking part of you with her. You still love her, Dante. Admit it.'

'You're right. She took something of mine, but

love?' He shook his head. 'I was dazzled, infatuated, but in the end it was just sex.'

Enough. He'd said enough. He had to go before he heard himself begging to stay and he took her hand, placed his key in her palm and closed her fingers around it. 'Take this.'

'But it's your key.'

'Now it is yours.' He bent to kiss her cheek and she leaned into him, drawn to him despite everything, and it took every ounce of self-control not to put his arms around her, hold her.

To his infinite regret, she'd seen him hold Valentina and it would be there, between them, until she could trust him, believe that he was hers, body and soul. He could show her in everything he did, but only she could choose to see.

'Dormi bene, mio amore. Sogui dolci.'

Something inside Geli screamed a long desperate *Noooooo!* as Dante turned and headed down the stairs. The hand he'd kissed reached out to him but he did not look back and when she heard him hit the lower flight, she closed the door and leaned back against it, clutching the key he'd given her.

'Now it is yours.' What did that mean?

That he had locked himself out until she invited him in? But this was his apartment... No, wait. This evening, when Valentina had asked him where the cats were, he'd said that they were in 'our apartment'. Not his, but *our* apartment. And Valentina hadn't batted an eyelid.

But she'd cried in his arms. And whispered something in Dante's ear before walking away.

What? What had she said to him? She tried making her lips form the words but it was hopeless.

She gave up, fetched a tub of ice cream from the freezer and ate it while the bath filled. Then she slid beneath the water and, letting its warmth seep into her, she blanked out Dante and his whole wretched family and did as he'd advised, focusing her entire mind on that moment when one of the world's most famous dress designers told her that her belt was 'quite perfect'.

She sprinkled a few drops of lavender oil on her pillow and then lay in bed and wrote down everything she could remember about the evening. What she'd worn down to the last stitch and stone—she should start keeping a clothes journal like her great-grandmother. She wrote how Dante had looked as he'd stood by the fire waiting for her because he was beautiful and she loved him and it was a memory to hold, cherish.

So much for nothing serious, not for keeps but for fun. If it had been that, then what had happened this evening would not have mattered.

So not like her mother...

She wrote everything she could remember about the limousine, about being snapped by the paparazzi as she'd walked the red carpet, the people she'd seen, every word that the Maestro had said to her.

Every word that Dante had said.

'Our' apartment. *'Our'* film...

His certainty that Valentina would not leave his father because she had everything she was looking for. If that was true, why had she been crying into his shoulder? Guilt, remorse...?

What had she whispered in Dante's ear?

It was the last thing she thought before *Dancing Queen* dragged her out of sleep.

Dante arrived on the dot of ten and they had a straightforward client/designer meeting downstairs in the room that was to be converted into an ice cream parlour, making final decisions about colours, furniture, artwork. They chose the ice cream cabinet and Dante used his laptop to go online and order it. Then he turned it around so that she could see a vintage jukebox he'd found.

'It plays old seventy-eights.'

'Boys' toys,' she muttered disapprovingly. 'It'll cost you a fortune to find records for it. And you won't get anyone later than...'

'Later than...?'

'I don't know. They pre-date my grandmother. Frank Sinatra?'

'That's a good start. See if you can find *Fly Me to the Moon*.'

She rolled her eyes but made a note then reached for her file as he picked it up to give it to her. Their hands met and, as he looked up, she might have forgotten herself, grabbed hold of him—

'I'll organise the decorators,' he said, standing up. 'Will you supervise them?'

'It's part of the job.' She checked her watch. 'If that's all, I have to go and change for lunch.'

The cleaning staff had been in. There were fresh flowers and a soft cat bed had been placed near the freshly lit fire, glowing behind the glass doors, for Mamma Cat and her kittens.

She checked on the cats, changed into her black minidress, topped it with the red velvet jacket that

Lisa had so admired and wore the laced boots from the night before. Her reflection suggested that it was too much.

It looked as if she was competing. She was at home and she should be more relaxed, informal, allow their guests to shine.

Our apartment…

She changed into narrow dark red velvet trousers and a black silk shirt which she topped with a long, dark red brocade waistcoat and ditched the boots for ballet flats.

Better. But, for the first time in her life, she wished her wardrobe contained at least one pink fluffy sweater. Because although she didn't want Dante to be right, deep down she knew he was.

She picked up his key and slipped it into the pocket of her waistcoat. It was a pledge of some sort. Of his sincerity, his commitment, maybe.

If only she knew what Valentina had whispered to him.

Her phoned beeped and, grateful for anything that would delay the moment when she'd have to go downstairs to the café, she picked it up and discovered a reply to the somewhat sharp message she'd sent to the bank.

Her balance had been restored, along with five

hundred pounds for her inconvenience. What? Banks didn't pay up like that unless they were being harassed by consumer programmes. Clearly they'd discovered some monumental error…

She had no excuse to stay now. Only the cats, but Matteo was desperate to give them a home.

She checked the clock. She couldn't put it off any longer. It was time to go, in every sense of the word.

She could hear Dante talking to someone on the phone as she passed his office. The door was slightly ajar; she didn't stop but she couldn't help wondering who he was talking to. That was how it was when you weren't sure. It was how Daniele must feel every day of his life but she couldn't live like that.

She was checking the table that had been set up in the corner when Dante joined her.

'Lunch first and then we'll go upstairs for coffee so that Valentina can meet the cats. Did the basket arrive?'

'Yes. Good thought. They'll look adorable.'

'If they're going to be on television they need more than a cardboard box…' He turned as the door opened and Valentina appeared in a gush of air kisses.

'*Ciao*, Geli. *Ciao*, Dante... Daniele had to park around the back somewhere. He's just coming. Can you get the door for him?'

Dante was calling out to Bruno behind the bar to bring water and menus as he opened the door so he didn't immediately see what was hampering his father.

Then he turned, looked down and saw Valentina's sleeping baby nestled in a softly padded buggy and in that moment Geli understood everything.

Valentina's tears, Daniele's uncertainty, Dante's grief.

He had not been mourning the loss of his love, but the child she had carried, given birth to and then placed in his father's arms.

In the excitement created by the arrival of the baby, the staff crowding around to coo over him, Geli reached out a hand to him and he grasped it so tightly that it hurt while he arranged his face into a smile.

Hours later—actually, it was no more than two but it had felt like a thousand—Geli shut the door behind their visitors and turned to Dante.

'Your father knows, doesn't he?' she said. 'That the baby is yours.'

'He had a fever when I was a child. That's when I first came to stay here with Nonnina. Valentina is his fourth wife but there have been no more children when, as you can see, he loves them...so I imagine there was some damage. I should have told you. I would have told you, but last night—'

'Don't...' She did not want to think about last night. That familiar, horrible sense of loss— 'We have known one another just over a week. Okay, we've probably spent more time together than some couples spend in months, but it's still new. We're still learning about one another. And that is a huge secret to share with anyone.'

'Secrets are poison. Valentina nearly fainted when she saw me last night. She was sure I was there to make trouble, to tell my father that Alberto isn't his child. Blow their lives apart.'

'Are you saying that she doesn't know that he knows?'

'Apparently not. That's when she cried, when I told her. With relief and joy, I think, to realise just how much he loved her.'

'I see.' And remembering the way Valentina had gone straight to her husband, put her arm in his—not a guilty wife returning to her husband's side, but one who knew how much she was loved—she did see.

'You asked me once if I regretted my choice, do you remember?'

'You said it was the wrong question. That I should be asking if you'd make the same decision again.' Could she ask it? Could she live with his answer... 'Would you?'

'The truth?'

'Parla come magni, caro.'

He smiled as she quoted his words back at him and her heart broke for him. After that first shocked moment he'd been so generous, admiring the baby, holding him, handing him back to his father to put in his buggy for a nap when it must have been tearing his heart out.

'There will always be regret, Angel, but a baby's place is with his mother and his mother's place is with the man who will make her happy. I can only hope that, should I be given the chance, I'd have the strength, the wisdom, the humanity to make the same decision.'

'You'd do that for them?'

'What should I do? Demand DNA tests? Give the readers of *Celebrità* a scandal to thrill them over the breakfast table? Make his mother the centre of vicious whispers?'

'No.' She shook her head. 'No…'

'I created a trust fund for Alberto when he was born, *cara*. And today, when you took Valentina to your workshop to show her your designs, Papà agreed to sign documents giving me legal access to Alberto, and to name me his guardian in the event of a divorce.'

'Will Valentina agree to that?'

'She knows that he will always be a part of my life,' he said. 'I want you to know that.'

'I treasure your trust. You are a very special man, Dante Vettori.' And to show her confidence, her trust, she took his key from her pocket and offered it to him.

'You are returning my key?'

'No, *caro*, I'm not returning it; I'm giving it to you for safe keeping.'

He took the key, put it in his pocket and then took her hand. 'I've missed you.'

'It was ten hours, Dante,' she said, stepping into his arm. 'But I've missed you, too.'

'Did I tell you that you look lovely today?'

'Make the most of it. I'm going to buy a pink fluffy jumper at the market on Tuesday. And if you don't kiss me right now, I'll wear it on television.'

His kiss was thorough and then, as a demonstration of how seriously he took her threat, he picked her up and carried her through to the bedroom and kissed every single part of her.

Later, when she was lying in his arms, he said, 'Tell me about this pink jumper thing. Is it going to be an ongoing threat? Not that I'm complaining.'

'I'll tell you when you can relax.' She looked up at him. 'Can I ask you a question?'

'Ask away.'

'What did Valentina whisper in your ear last night?'

'You saw?'

'I saw.'

'She said, *"Si prega di essere felice..."* I'd told her that I'd met someone and, having met you, she was urging me to be happy.' He leaned down and kissed her. 'A command that I'm delighted to obey.'

'Uh-oh.'

'Cara?'

'I've had a text from Elle. I knew opening

the ice cream parlour at Easter was a mistake. They're all coming to see it.'

'They're flying to Milan to see an ice cream parlour?'

'Professional interest?' she offered.

'Cara...'

'Okay, they're coming to check you out. Sorry, I've tried to be as casual about us as I can be, but the less you say, the more big sisters read between the lines.'

'Is there anything I should know? Topics not to be mentioned?'

'Just be yourself and they'll love you. But I have to find somewhere for them to stay.'

'I'll call Papà and ask if the villa at Lake Como is going to be free.'

'It's not. Valentina told me that they're going to the Lake for Easter. She rang to invite us while you were out. I thought that maybe we could go down on Sunday for the day so that you can spend time with Alberto but...'

'But nothing. There's plenty of room.' He took out his phone. 'Four adults, three children, one baby, right?' She nodded and he made the call. 'They're delighted to have them and we'll stay over until Tuesday. It'll give you plenty of time to catch up with your sisters.'

'Did I ever tell you that I love you?' she said.

'Not since breakfast. Are we done here?'

She looked around at the rich green walls, the huge brilliant print—just the corner of an ice cream sundae with all the focus on a huge, glistening red cherry—the white-painted furniture, vintage jukebox and gleaming ice cream counter waiting to be filled.

Outside in the courtyard, tubs of red and white flowers were overflowing from old stone troughs and she'd threaded tiny white solar-powered fairy lights through the vines that would light up as dusk fell.

'It looks done to me.'

'Then come with me. I have something to show you.'

He took her outside and unlocked the front door of the tall narrow building next door that had, until the owner retired a few weeks ago, been a hardware store.

'More expansion plans?' she asked. 'Only I'm a bit busy.'

She'd been working flat out since the photograph of her talking to the Maestro had appeared in an Italian lifestyle magazine reporting his interest in her belt. Now it seemed everyone wanted one.

He had offered her a job in return for the rights to reproduce it but, flattered as she was, she didn't want to be a nameless designer producing ideas for a designer 'brand'.

She had her own label and was collaborating with a student who could do amazing things with leather to produce variations on her design in gorgeous colours.

She'd also had an order for a dozen of her spider web beaded silk chiffon tops for a Milan boutique.

'I know how busy you are and that you need more space,' he said. 'Welcome to your *atelier*.'

'What? No...'

'No?' Dante repeated. 'You do not think this would make appropriate showroom space for your designs?'

'A showroom...' She spun around, imagining everything painted white, shelves, a display table, one brilliantly coloured piece in the small window. 'You know it's perfect.'

'I'm glad that's settled. There's a room out the back for office and storage and two rooms on the next floor for workshop space. And on the top floor...'

She turned to him, knowing what was coming. She'd told him, that first night in Isola, about her dream. A house with three floors. One for sales, one for work and one to live in.

'There's a little apartment. Just big enough for one?'

'Well, it's a bit bigger than that. I thought we could knock it through.'

She frowned. 'Knock it through? I don't understand. Have you bought this?'

'No. At least not recently. I inherited some money from my maternal grandfather when I turned twenty-one and Nonnina wanted to raise the money to help her son set up in business in Australia. She owned the whole block and it seemed like a good investment, even if part of the deal was that she stayed on, rent-free, until she decided to retire. Papà would buy it in a heartbeat if it was for sale.'

'*Madonna*, Dante, you know how to take the wind out of a girl's sails.'

He shrugged. 'So you're good with that? Extending the apartment? Only we'll need more space when we're married.'

And, while she was struggling to get her chin under control, he produced a small leather box from his pocket and opened it to reveal a large solitaire diamond.

'Dante, *caro*, my love, are you sure? There's no hurry…'

He did not pretend that he did not understand but said, 'This is different in so many ways from Valentina. We are not just lovers, Angel, we're friends. *Siete la mia aria…* You are the air I breathe. *Voglio stare con te per sempre…* I want to stay with you for ever. *Ti amo.*' And then again in English, so there could be no mistake. 'I love you, *mia amore.* I would leave here and go to the ends of the earth to be with you.'

She dashed away a tear, took the ring from the box and gave it to him, holding out her hand, and as he placed it on her finger she said, '*Siete la mia aria,* Dante. *Voglio stare con te per sempre…* I would live in a cave with you.'

There were two weddings. The first was in Isola early in May. They said their vows in the *muni-*

cipio, with Giovanni standing as his best man and his own bride, Lisa, as her very best woman. Afterwards everyone was invited to a party in the communal garden. The feast was lavish but still everyone brought something they had made to add to the table. Geli's family returned to Isola for the occasion, bringing with them her grandmother and Great-Uncle Basil. Nonnina flew with her son from Australia to be with Dante and meet his bride. A fiddler played so that they could dance and later, as dusk fell, a jazz quartet filled the air with smooth, mellow music while the square was lit up with thousands of tiny white fairy lights.

Six weeks later, in midsummer, Geli and Dante repeated their vows in the Orangery at Haughton Manor, just as Geli's sister had done a few years earlier, followed by a picnic in the park with Rosie in attendance to provide all the ice cream anyone could eat. This time her sisters were her best women, her small nieces her bridesmaids and Great-Uncle Basil gave her away.

Over the vintage cream slipper satin vintage gown she'd adapted for both occasions, Geli wore a luscious new belt made from shocking-pink suede, which made the front page of *Celebrità* and its English version, *Celebrity*.

An order book for a limited edition of the design was filled the same day.

* * * * *

MILLS & BOON®
Large Print – November 2015

The Ruthless Greek's Return
Sharon Kendrick

Bound by the Billionaire's Baby
Cathy Williams

Married for Amari's Heir
Maisey Yates

A Taste of Sin
Maggie Cox

Sicilian's Shock Proposal
Carol Marinelli

Vows Made in Secret
Louise Fuller

The Sheikh's Wedding Contract
Andie Brock

A Bride for the Italian Boss
Susan Meier

The Millionaire's True Worth
Rebecca Winters

The Earl's Convenient Wife
Marion Lennox

Vettori's Damsel in Distress
Liz Fielding

MILLS & BOON®
Large Print – December 2015

The Greek Demands His Heir
Lynne Graham

The Sinner's Marriage Redemption
Annie West

His Sicilian Cinderella
Carol Marinelli

Captivated by the Greek
Julia James

The Perfect Cazorla Wife
Michelle Smart

Claimed for His Duty
Tara Pammi

The Marakaios Baby
Kate Hewitt

Return of the Italian Tycoon
Jennifer Faye

His Unforgettable Fiancée
Teresa Carpenter

Hired by the Brooding Billionaire
Kandy Shepherd

A Will, a Wish...a Proposal
Jessica Gilmore

MILLS & BOON®

Why shop at millsandboon.co.uk?

Each year, thousands of romance readers find their perfect read at millsandboon.co.uk. That's because we're passionate about bringing you the very best romantic fiction. Here are some of the advantages of shopping at www.millsandboon.co.uk:

* **Get new books first**—you'll be able to buy your favourite books one month before they hit the shops

* **Get exclusive discounts**—you'll also be able to buy our specially created monthly collections, with up to 50% off the RRP

* **Find your favourite authors**—latest news, interviews and new releases for all your favourite authors and series on our website, plus ideas for what to try next

* **Join in**—once you've bought your favourite books, don't forget to register with us to rate, review and join in the discussions

Visit **www.millsandboon.co.uk**
for all this and more today!